RABBITS ON THE RUN

There was a brown envelope on the table. Lydia took a letter out of it. 'It's from Walton Borough Council,' she said.

Mandy frowned. *Why on earth was the council writing to Lydia?*

Lydia explained: 'Sam Western has applied for a court order to allow him to shoot our rabbits.'

'He can't!' John spluttered. 'Not if they're on *your* land!'

'Apparently he can,' Lydia said in a shaky voice. 'The court order will take effect from next Monday.'

John gasped. 'That's only five days away!'

Animal Ark series

LUCY DANIELS

Rabbits

— *on the* —

Run

Illustrations by Jenny Gregory

*Hodder
Children's
Books*

a division of Hodder Headline plc

Special thanks to Sue Welford
Thanks also C. J. Hall, B.Vet.Med., M.R.C.V.S., for reviewing the
veterinary information contained in this book.

Text copyright © 1998 Ben M. Baglio
Created by Ben M. Baglio, London W12 7QY
Illustrations copyright © 1998 Jenny Gregory

First published in Great Britain in 1998
by Hodder Children's Books

A Catalogue record for this book is available from the British Library

ISBN 0 340 72401 3

Typeset by Avon Dataset Ltd, Bidford-on-Avon, Warks

Printed and bound in Great Britain by
Clays Ltd, St Ives plc

Hodder Children's Books
a division of Hodder Headline plc
338 Euston Road
London NW1 3BH

One

'How can anyone be so horrible?' Mandy Hope said in a loud voice. She was perched on the edge of the armchair eating her lunch-time sandwich. She sat bolt upright, seething with indignation as she watched a television programme about animal welfare. It showed a helper at an animal rescue centre caring for a young German shepherd. The dog had been abandoned and had big, melting brown eyes that seemed to reflect the misery of its short life. It looked half-starved, its tawny coat a mess of matted fur.

'Poor thing!' Mandy called out to her mother in the kitchen. 'Mum, come and see!'

Emily Hope came in, carrying a glass of cola for Mandy in one hand and a mug of tea in the other. She sat down beside her daughter. Mandy's parents were both veterinary surgeons in the Yorkshire village of Welford. The Animal Ark surgery had a residential unit for sick animals at the back and was attached to the family's house, an old, low-roofed, stone cottage.

Mrs Hope was grabbing a quick lunch-break in the middle of her busy day's schedule. She shook her head in sympathy at the animal on the screen. 'Oh dear,' she murmured.

Mandy stretched out her hand for her glass without taking her eyes off the television. 'Thanks, Mum. Honestly, that dog's owner should be shot.'

'If you had your way, love, everyone that mistreats animals would be shot,' her mum said, with a wry smile.

'And quite right too!' Mandy still seethed with anger. 'Thank goodness for those rescue centres; they do a really brilliant job.' She took a sip of her drink. 'If I wasn't going to be a vet when I'm older, I'd like to work somewhere like that.'

Mrs Hope put her arm round her daughter's shoulders and gave her a quick hug. 'I'm sure you're doing your bit already, love.'

It was true. Mandy and her best friend, James Hunter, were always helping animals in trouble. James was a year younger than Mandy and loved animals almost as much as she did.

'Yes, I suppose so.' Mandy sighed and took another gulp of cola as the programme finished and the credits rolled up the screen.

Her mum pushed back a wisp of Mandy's fair hair that had fallen over her eyes. 'So, what are you and James going to do with yourselves the rest of this school holiday?'

'Oh, we've got lots of plans,' Mandy said.

Mandy and James had spent the first few days of the holiday helping Mrs Hunter decorate James's bedroom. Now it was finished, they had other things to do.

Mrs Hope laughed. 'I bet. You two never sit still.' She finished her tea and got up to look out of the window. It was early autumn and already the leaves were beginning to fall. 'It's stopped raining, thank goodness,' she said.

A sharp burst of sun between the broken clouds framed Mrs Hope's red hair with light. She spotted a figure coming down the lane. 'Oh, and here *is* James.' She chuckled. 'It looks as if Blackie's taking *him* for a walk.' Blackie was James's Labrador dog.

Mandy jumped up and rushed out into the kitchen. 'Oh dear, James won't be very happy. I was supposed to be calling for *him*. That programme made me forget the time.'

'And here's Dad too.' Mrs Hope followed Mandy out as the Animal Ark Land-rover came bouncing down the lane past James. 'I'd better get a move on. I'm taking surgery this afternoon.'

Mandy was hurriedly rinsing her glass under the tap. 'We promised Lydia we'd help her to repair Houdini's shelter,' she told her mum. 'It almost collapsed in that gale we had last week and she hasn't been able to repair it on her own.'

'That's very kind of you both,' Mrs Hope said.

'Oh, we love going up to High Cross.' Mandy had a soft spot for Houdini, a billy-goat belonging to Lydia Fawcett, the owner of High Cross Farm.

Lydia had helped Mandy, James and their friend John Hardy save a colony of rabbits that lived on a strip of land between her farm and Upper Welford Hall. The owner of the Hall, wealthy farmer Sam Western, had wanted to shoot the rabbits, but Lydia had saved them by proving the land belonged to her. She had ordered Sam Western and his men to keep away.

The trouble was, by protecting the rabbits, Lydia had made an enemy of Sam Western. He wasn't used to losing battles and Mandy had always had the horrible feeling he'd try to get his own back one day.

'That's great,' Mrs Hope said when Mandy told her they were going up to High Cross to help Lydia. She rummaged in the dresser drawer for something to tie back her hair.

'And then we're doing advanced training with Blackie,' Mandy went on.

'*Advanced!* You've got to be joking!' The back door opened and Adam Hope came in just in time to hear what Mandy said. 'Blackie hasn't even passed the novice stage yet, and I've just seen him dragging James off in the opposite direction to where he wants to go,' he said with a grin on his face. 'Poor old James, he was trying to steer his bike *and* drag Blackie backwards at the same time. I've got a terrible feeling Blackie won.'

'Oh, Adam!' Mrs Hope laughed.

Mandy looked indignant at first, but then she laughed too. 'Don't be so rotten, Dad. James would be very hurt if he heard you say that about Blackie not being trained.' She peered out of the kitchen window. She wondered what had happened to James. Maybe Blackie had dragged him all the way back to the village green. Once Blackie got an idea in his head there was no stopping him!

Mr Hope put his vet's bag down on the kitchen table and plonked himself in a chair

with a huge sigh. 'What a morning! Difficult calving at Woodbridge Farm. Twins. Mr Marsh was in a real state.'

'*Mr Marsh* was? What about the poor mother cow?' Mrs Hope asked.

'Oh, she was OK . . . after I'd helped her out with a bit of pulling and shoving,' Mr Hope replied.

Mandy came and put her arms on her dad's shoulders. She gave him a hug. 'Good old Dad,' she said. 'What would the farmers of Welford do without you?'

'No idea.' Adam Hope grinned broadly.

'The kettle's hot if you want a cup of tea,' Emily Hope told her husband, as she took her white vet's coat from the back of the door and pulled it on.

Mr Hope glanced at the clock on the mantelpiece above the stove, where it sat amidst an untidy assortment of letters, bills, notes, a chipped blue mug full of pens and a framed photo of Mandy when she was a toddler. He shook his head. 'No thanks, I haven't got time. I only popped in to say hi. I'm off out again in a minute – to Bennetts' stables. They've a horse that's gone lame.'

'Not Matty?' Mandy asked in alarm. The gentle grey mare was Mandy's favourite at Bennetts' Riding Stables, where she and James had learned to ride.

'No, it's not Matty,' her father replied, smiling. 'I think Wilfred mentioned that it was Star.'

'Oh. Poor Star.' Mandy was relieved that Matty wasn't ill, but Star was a sweetie, too.

'Right, then,' Mrs Hope said. 'It's Simon's afternoon off, so I'd better get in there. There's probably a queue already.' Simon was the veterinary nurse.

Mrs Hope dropped a kiss on top of Mandy's head. 'See you later. Have a nice afternoon.'

'See you,' Mandy said absent-mindedly. Where on earth *was* James?

Mr Hope had followed his wife through the door that led from the cottage into the back of the surgery. 'I've got to look at the results of those blood samples from Mrs Dyson's cat,' Mandy heard her mum say. 'I'm pretty sure he's anaemic, but I hope it's nothing worse.'

Then a knock came at the back door. When Mandy opened it she saw James standing there, red-faced and looking flustered.

'What happened to you?' he demanded. 'You were supposed to be coming over to my house.'

'Sorry,' Mandy apologised. She explained about the animal programme. 'And what happened to *you*?' she asked, eyeing him up and down.

'I would have been here sooner but Blackie had other ideas.' James's glasses were steamed up and he was still trying to catch his breath.

Mandy bent to say hello to the Labrador. He jumped up and licked her face, his tail wagging so hard it was just a dark blur. 'Mum saw you coming down the lane then you completely disappeared,' she said to James.

'Blackie spotted Mrs Ponsonby with Pandora and Toby,' he explained. 'And he hared off like a maniac to say hello.'

Bossy Mrs Ponsonby lived at Bleakfell Hall, a huge, rambling, Victorian house just outside

Welford. She often walked her dogs through the village.

'Then I met John Hardy,' James went on. 'His school holiday has just started.' John was the same age as James, but went to boarding-school in the Lake District so he was only around during his school holidays. His dad Julian and his stepmother Sara ran the Fox and Goose, Welford's pub.

'Oh, good!' Mandy exclaimed. She had really got to know John properly when they had rescued Lydia's wild rabbits. 'How is he?'

By now James had recovered his breath. 'He's fine. I told him we were going to see Lydia and he asked if he could come with us. He wants to see how her rabbits are doing.'

'Right.' Mandy grabbed her coat from the hook behind the door and pushed her feet into her wellingtons. 'We'll call for him first, then.'

They collected their bikes, wheeling them down the brick path, past the wooden sign that said 'Animal Ark: Veterinary Surgery' then set off up the lane that led to the village green.

It was a breezy autumn afternoon with bright

bursts of sunshine through grey clouds that scudded across the sky. The village green was scattered with golden leaves as Mandy, James and Blackie passed through on their way to the Fox and Goose.

When they got there John was sitting on one of the outside benches, waiting for them. His bike was propped up against the side of the stone porch that led into the bar.

'Hi, Mandy. Hi, James!' he called.

'Hi, John, it's great to see you.' Mandy eyed John's camera slung round his neck. 'You're still keen on taking photos, then?' John had taken lots of pictures of Lydia's rabbits in the summer.

John took the camera out of its case to show them. 'This is a new one. It's got an advanced system and I'm dying to try it out.'

'It looks a bit complicated.' James peered at the large lens with all its numbers and symbols.

John grinned, 'It's pretty easy really,' he said. 'Shall we go? I can't wait to see if Lydia's rabbits are all right.'

'Lydia's rabbits?' A loud voice came from the porch and Sam Western came out with a frown on his face. He was a big, bluff man wearing a green waxed jacket and shiny brown leather boots. 'What about them?'

Mandy drew in her breath. She knew the word 'rabbit' was like a red rag to a bull to Sam Western. He hated them. To him they were just eating machines, chomping at his fruit bushes, nibbling at his crops. Every plant cost money to grow and anything that cost Sam Western money had to be guarded as if it was the crown jewels!

'Er . . . we're just going up to High Cross to see how they're doing,' Mandy told him.

'Oh, *I* can tell you how they're doing,' Sam Western told them angrily. 'They're doing very well – eating *my* crops!' He leaned forward. 'If you're going up to that Lydia woman's place you can give her a message from me.'

Mandy's heart turned over. She knew that when Sam Western had that angry look on his face, it meant trouble. Real trouble.

'What message?' she asked calmly, even though her heart was thudding like a drum.

'You can tell her those wretched rabbits' days are numbered,' Mr Western said.

'What do you mean?' James asked indignantly.

'She'll find out soon enough,' Sam Western called over his shoulder, as he strode round to the carpark at the back of the building.

Mandy, James and John looked at one another in dismay.

'What do you think he meant?' Mandy asked in a small voice. She suddenly felt worried. Very worried indeed.

John shook his head. 'I don't know, but I reckon we should get up to High Cross and tell Lydia as fast as we can.' He jumped on his bike and set off, pedalling as quickly as he could.

The other two sped after him.

'I don't know why you're so worried, John,' James panted as they caught him up. 'Mr Western can't harm the rabbits. They live on Lydia's land, not his.'

'I know,' John said. 'But I've got a horrible feeling he's got something up his sleeve.'

Mandy nodded in agreement. 'The sooner we warn Lydia, the better.'

Two

They arrived at Lydia's farm out of breath. High Cross Farm was a ramshackle smallholding perched on the side of a hill near the Beacon. All around were hawthorns, bent and twisted into peculiar shapes by the bitter winds that blew in from the north on cold winter days.

Lydia's farmhouse looked neglected and the garden was so overgrown it seemed as if no one had tended it for years. But the yard and goat shelters, though dilapidated, were spick and span and, inside, the old-fashioned farmhouse kitchen was warm and cosy from a stove that Lydia kept going, winter and summer.

The front door was ajar. Inside, Lydia was just piling logs into a basket by the stove. She looked startled when Mandy knocked on the door and peered in.

'Hi, Lydia, can we come in?'

When she saw who it was, Lydia's weather-worn face broke into a broad smile and she beckoned them inside. 'Come in, come in,' she said. 'And how nice to see you too, John,' she added, when she saw who Mandy and James had brought with them. 'How are you?'

'Oh, Lydia,' Mandy burst out before John could reply. 'You'll never guess what's hap-pened. We've just seen Sam Western and he—'

'He's got something up his sleeve about the rabbits,' John interrupted.

'And he said to tell you their days are numbered,' James added, as he tried to stop Blackie putting his nose into a tray full of fresh scones that Lydia had just taken out of the oven. 'Blackie!' he growled. 'Sit!'

'Now, now, calm down, you three,' Lydia said. Her baggy old trousers flapped round her ankles as she bustled about finding them lemonade from the larder. She put four scones on a plate and made them all sit down at the table.

'Right. Now,' she said, when they were all seated. 'Take a deep breath and tell me what all this is about.'

Mandy told Lydia quickly about their encounter with Sam Western.

'And you know he doesn't make idle threats,' she added. 'Oh, Lydia, what do you think he's going to do?'

Lydia ran her hand through her cropped hair and looked thoughtful. Then she shook her head. 'There's nothing he *can* do,' she said. 'He's just trying to scare me, that's all. I've already told him he can't come on my land to deal with the rabbits. You know he hated losing that battle over them before. I knew he wouldn't let it rest. But he still can't do anything.'

James took a bite of his scone. 'I told them not to panic,' he said with his mouth full.

John hadn't touched his scone, or his

lemonade. 'How *are* the rabbits, anyway?' he asked anxiously.

'Thriving,' Lydia smiled. 'Would you like to go and see them?'

'Oh, yes please,' John replied.

Mandy lagged behind as John and James hurriedly ate their scones and finished their drinks and went outside with Lydia. She simply couldn't dismiss Sam Western's threat just like that.

In the yard, she stood in front of Houdini's shelter, looking at the storm damage. The corrugated iron roof was leaning at a crazy angle and one side was coming apart. It certainly did need a lot of repair. She sighed. Lydia really didn't have a lot of money to spare for new timber.

Houdini was in his paddock looking at Mandy over the chain link fence. She went across to talk to him.

'Hi, Houdini.' She tugged gently at his jet black, shiny forelock. Houdini had a special place in her heart. He bleated gently and stared at her with his emerald eyes. Mandy loved goats as much as Sam Western hated them. She knew that, to him, goats were almost as bad as rabbits. Especially Houdini, who had once escaped and broken into the garden at Upper Welford Hall and tucked into a meal of Mr Western's precious plants.

'Come on, Mandy,' James called. They were already crossing the goat paddock and heading for the meadow where the rabbits could usually be found. Lydia's other goats came running as soon as everyone appeared, nuzzling sleeves and pockets for titbits, bleating as they tried to push in front of one another.

Mandy caught up with the others as they climbed the stile into the far meadow that bordered Sam Western's property. In the spring it was full of wild flowers: buttercups, ox-eye daisies, milkmaids and tall, rust-coloured spikes of sorrel. One side bordered the garden of Upper Welford Hall and the far end sloped down towards Sam Western's maize field. Usually it was alive with rabbits. But today, strangely, there were none.

James and John stood there staring. Blackie pulled at his lead and sniffed the air. Surely they hadn't come all the way up to High Cross and there wasn't even a *smell* of a rabbit?

John looked disappointed. 'Where *are* they?' he said.

Suddenly, as he spoke, a loud bang sounded from the other side of Sam Western's field. Then another, and another. Everyone gazed at Lydia in horror.

'Someone's shooting!' John blurted out, his eyes wide with fright.

Lydia nodded and sighed. 'It's Sam Western's men. They're shooting the rabbits in his field, I'm afraid.'

'How can they be so mean?' Mandy said angrily.

Lydia shook her head. 'I'm afraid Mr Western can do what he likes on his own land.'

'But at least he can't shoot *your* rabbits,' James said.

Lydia gave him a wan smile. 'That's right. He can't.'

'You are sure yours are all right, aren't you?'

John was still looking round anxiously. 'I still can't see any.'

'Yes,' Lydia said. 'Don't you worry. If we're quiet they'll soon come out.'

And, as she spoke, a black twitchy nose appeared. Then another, and another. And soon a dozen or so rabbits could be seen running, hopping, skipping and lolloping across the meadow – the older ones first, sniffing the air for danger, then the younger ones, velvet ears twitching and snowball tails bobbing.

'Oh,' Mandy breathed. 'Aren't they gorgeous?'

John stood beside her, still as a statue. 'They're brilliant.' He put his camera to his eye, adjusted the lens and clicked the shutter.

There must have been thirty or forty grey and tawny rabbits of all shapes and sizes. There were the big males, smaller females, and lots of youngsters. This had once been a nursery warren. Mandy spotted a really large rabbit that she felt sure must be their leader. He was magnificent: sitting bolt upright, huge dark eyes bright, ears twitching, his noble head outlined against the backdrop of maize. But he didn't know anyone was watching. The rabbits were upwind and no human smell came to disturb them.

Several rabbits had large cobs of corn in their mouths. Mandy winced as she realised that the rabbits were returning from Sam Western's cornfield. He'd be furious if he saw them. They scrambled down their holes and into the maze of underground tunnels that made up their colony. Their powerful back legs kicked out as they disappeared from sight.

Mandy turned again to the big rabbit sitting alert on a tussock of grass. His fur glinted in the sun. She drew in her breath as he sat up on his hind legs and began to comb his ears with his front paws. 'Look at him,' she breathed. 'I bet he's their king.'

James chuckled. 'King Rabbit . . . I like that.'

'They're certainly having a feast on that maize,' Lydia whispered.

All round the warren and along the fence Mandy could see a scattering of shiny, golden corncobs, their surrounding leaves dried and

withered. The crop was ripe and soon Mr Western's great combine harvester would come to cut it. She imagined the huge green machine cutting a swathe through the maize and spewing the shredded plants out of its chute and into the waiting trailers. The harvest would be stored in one of the barns at Upper Welford Hall and used to make silage for cattle feed in the winter.

Lydia sighed. 'I can see why Sam Western is annoyed,' she admitted. 'After all, he grows the maize to feed his cattle, not the rabbits.'

'But there aren't *that* many rabbits living in your field,' John argued. 'The amount they eat from the neighbouring field can't really make much difference . . . can it?' Even John sounded unsure.

Mandy had a horrible sinking feeling. The rabbits might have their warren on Lydia's land, but they were trespassing on to Mr Western's field to eat his crops. Maybe there *was* something he could do about it after all. And if there was, Sam Western wouldn't be afraid to do it. They'd already heard his men shooting rabbits that were unlucky enough to be caught stealing his crops on other parts of his land.

They watched the rabbits playing in the sun for a while then Lydia said, 'Come on. Let's leave them to it, shall we?'

Mandy tried to shake off her feeling of dread as they turned reluctantly, climbed the stile and began to make their way back across the goat paddock. Sam Western was up to something and she wished she knew what it was.

The goats had gathered round the gate, bleating and tossing their heads.

'Milking time,' Lydia announced, as she strode on ahead. 'They're as regular as clockwork, my girls.' She went indoors to wash her hands reading for milking.

'We really came to help you mend Houdini's shelter,' Mandy said, as they followed her inside, suddenly remembering the main purpose of their visit.

'Oh,' Lydia said. 'That's very kind of you. But perhaps you could come back another time? I think it's safe enough for now.'

'Yes, I'm sure we can,' Mandy replied.

'What shall we do now?' James asked, as Lydia headed off to the dairy.

'I'd like to take some more pictures before we go home,' John put in.

Lydia came out with a bundle of goat halters in her hands. She had heard what John said. 'Why don't you go up to Longstone Edge?' she suggested. 'You get a lovely view up there, especially since the Forestry Commission cut some of the trees down.'

'Cut the trees down?' James asked curiously. 'What for?'

'They've been coppicing the ash and chestnut trees,' Lydia told them. 'The wood needed thinning out to let in some light, and the timber's valuable for fencing and hurdle-making. They'll grow again, don't worry.'

John looked at the others. 'Shall we go up there, then?'

'If you like.' Mandy and James agreed.

They left Lydia collecting the goats and headed off. Leaving their bikes by the stile, they climbed over and walked round the edge of the next field.

Mandy's mind was still on the rabbits as they tramped along, past the Beacon and towards Longstone Edge. John was also very quiet. Mandy knew he was worrying about them too.

James had let Blackie off the lead and he bounded on ahead, sniffing every tree trunk, every clump of grass that he came across.

The footpath crossed a stream that bubbled its way down to the river in the valley. Mandy tried to push Sam Western's threat to the back of her mind as they jumped from stone to stone until they were on dry land again. Longstone Edge was straight ahead. The tyre tracks of the tractors and trailers used by the forestry workers were still clearly visible along the unmade road that led into the wood.

Blackie galloped on ahead, leaping over the stile beside the foresters' gate, splashing along through the muddy puddles and clumps of marsh grass into the clearing where the trees had been felled. The stumps looked strange – all sorts of weird shapes and sizes. Piles of sawdust were evidence of the foresters' chainsaws. In spring, the stumps would shoot back into life, sending up slender wands of new growth, and the wood would be green and shady again.

John wandered off. He stood up on one of the tree stumps and took a long shot of the path through the wood. Then he walked on, focusing the camera on a shaft of sunlight shining through the trees.

James threw a stick for Blackie. The dog bounded after it, crashing through a clump of brambles, sniffing around, his tail waving like a banner. He found the stick and ran off with it in the opposite direction. Then he dropped it and began to dig, his strong front paws sending showers of earth shooting into the air.

'Blackie!' James ran to drag him away before he got covered in mud.

Mandy caught up with John. He was standing gazing over the moorland. He took a photo of the view, then turned to Mandy. She could tell from his face that he was still thinking about Sam Western's message to Lydia. 'I'm still sure that man's planning something,' he said unhappily.

'So am I,' Mandy agreed with a sigh. 'I only wish I knew what.'

By now, James had dragged Blackie away from the hole he was digging and the Labrador had run off into the part of the wood where the trees hadn't been cut. Through the lacework of branches they could see the sun beginning to go down. Mandy realised it was time they were getting back.

'Come on, you two,' she called to the boys. 'John can take some more pictures tomorrow.'

The light was beginning to fade as they headed home. At the crossroads by the Fox and Goose they said goodbye to John. Mandy and James split up by the green and Mandy headed off down the lane towards Animal Ark.

Indoors, Emily Hope was preparing the evening meal, while Adam Hope took early evening surgery.

Mrs Hope glanced up as Mandy came through the door. 'Had a nice afternoon, love?'

Mandy plonked herself down at the kitchen table. 'Not really,' she said with a sigh.

Her mum stopped chopping carrots. 'Why? What's wrong?'

Mandy told her quickly what Sam Western had said.

'Oh dear,' Mrs Hope sighed. 'But try not to worry about it, Mandy. At least until you find out exactly what he meant.'

Mandy sighed too. 'I know. But I just can't help it.'

Her mum smiled and put her arm round Mandy's shoulders. 'Come on, love, cheer up. It may not be as bad as you think.'

Mandy managed a smile too. But inside she was still worried. If only there was a way to find out what Sam Western was planning she might feel a whole lot better.

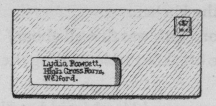

Lydia Fawcett,
High Cross Farm,
Welford.

Three

It was early the following morning. Mandy was just coming down the stairs when the phone rang.

'I'll get it!' She jumped down the last four steps and picked up the receiver.

'Mandy, can you and your friends come up here right away? I'm afraid I've got some bad news.' It was Lydia. She sounded almost in tears.

Mandy's heart turned over. 'Lydia! What is it?'

'I don't want to tell you over the phone. I'll tell you when you get here,' Lydia insisted.

Mandy quickly phoned James and John, then ran into the kitchen.

'What on earth was that all about?' Mr Hope was at the breakfast table reading the morning paper.

'An emergency,' Mandy said breathlessly.

Her dad frowned. 'An emergency? For me?'

Mandy shook her head. 'No, me . . . and James and John. We've got to go up to High Cross.'

'What kind of an emergency is it?' her dad asked.

'I'm not sure.' Mandy grabbed a piece of toast with one hand and took a bite while pulling her jacket from the back of the door with the other. 'See you later, Dad.'

Mr Hope sighed, shook his head and went back to his newspaper.

At the end of the lane Mandy spotted James racing across the green on his bike. They hurried over to John, who was waiting for them on the High Street.

'What do you think's wrong?' James panted as they sped towards High Cross.

Mandy shook her head. 'I don't know but it sounded pretty urgent.'

At High Cross, Lydia opened the door when she saw them coming through the gate.

'Come in, my dears,' she said, shaking her head. 'I don't know what you're going to say when I tell you what's happened.'

There was a brown envelope on the table. Lydia took a letter out of it. 'It's from Walton Borough Council,' she said.

Mandy frowned. *Why on earth was the Council writing to Lydia?*

Lydia explained: 'Sam Western has applied for a court order to allow him to shoot our rabbits.'

'But he can't!' John spluttered. 'They're on *your* land!'

'Apparently he can,' Lydia replied sadly. She read out loud from the letter: ' "Under the Pest Act of 1947 you are obliged to control rabbits that live on your land. As this is not being done, permission will be given to Mr Western to enter your property to destroy them." ' She sighed, and sat down heavily at her table.

'Pest Act?' James exclaimed. 'What's that?'

'It's the name of a special law made to control animals or insects that are causing a nuisance,' Lydia said in a shaky voice. 'The court order will take effect from next Monday.'

John gasped. 'That's only five days away!'

James was looking stunned. 'He can't, he really can't.'

Lydia shook her head sadly. 'I'm sorry, James. I'm afraid it looks as if he can.'

'We've got to stop him!' Mandy cried.

Lydia was still shaking her head. 'I don't see

how. Mr Western's got the law on his side. I'm afraid there's nothing we can do.'

But Mandy refused to be put off. 'Dad's got a lawyer friend in Walton,' she said. 'I'll get him to phone and ask if there's any way we can stop the court order. He'll know, I'm sure.' She turned to the others. 'Come on, let's get back.'

At Animal Ark, Mr Hope was busy in morning surgery. There was nothing to do but wait until he had finished. Mandy, James and John sat round the kitchen table looking unhappy.

'We can't just let him go and shoot all those rabbits,' James said.

Mandy bit her lip. 'Let's wait and find out what Dad's friend says,' she insisted.

Luckily, it wasn't long before Mr Hope came through into the kitchen for a quick coffee-break. He looked surprised to see three anxious faces gazing at him as he came through the door.

'A reception committee?' he grinned, then his face fell when he saw how upset they were. 'What's wrong?' he asked.

Mandy quickly explained about the court order. 'So will you please phone your lawyer friend to ask if there's any way we can stop it?' she pleaded.

Mr Hope sighed and sat down beside them. 'Look, you three,' he said gently. 'You've already had one battle over those rabbits. Don't you think you'd better leave well enough alone this time?'

'Dad!' Mandy blurted out indignantly. 'How can you say such a thing!'

Mr Hope held up his hands. 'OK, OK, I suppose I should know better. But honestly, Mandy, a court order is a court order. I doubt there'll be anything you can do about it.'

'But *please* ring your friend, just to make sure,' Mandy insisted.

Mr Hope sighed again. 'OK.' He rose and went out into the hall to use the phone. Mandy's heart was beating like a drum. She had a horrible feeling she wasn't going to like what her dad's friend had to say one little bit.

Mr Hope came back looking grim. 'I'm sorry,

love. It doesn't look as if there's anything you can do.'

Mandy looked at James and John in dismay. 'Oh, Dad! Why not?' she exclaimed.

'Apparently Lydia *could* fight the court order, but an appeal would cost her quite a lot in legal fees,' Mr Hope explained.

Mandy shook her head. 'She couldn't afford anything like that.'

Mr Hope shook his head. 'And there's no denying that those rabbits are eating Sam Western's crops. I doubt she'd have a leg to stand on.' He looked round at their stricken faces. 'So . . . I'm afraid this is one battle you three just aren't going to win.'

Mandy felt tears prick the back of her eyelids. They couldn't give up just like that. There simply *had* to be something they could do.

Four

James had promised to weed the garden for his mum and John was going into Walton with his dad and Sara, so once Mr Hope had gone back to work, Mandy was left alone at Animal Ark.

She was gazing out of the front window and racking her brains for ideas to save the rabbits when she spotted Ernie Bell coming down the lane towards Animal Ark carrying a cat basket.

Mr Bell lived in one of the tiny cottages behind the Fox and Goose and was an old friend of Mandy's grandad. They had both lived in Welford all their lives and were bell-ringers at the church. Other people might think Ernie gruff and grumpy but Mandy knew better. If they saw him with his beloved cat and his pet squirrel, Sammy, they would know that inside he was as soft as fudge.

'Hi, Mr Bell,' she said, going outside to meet him. She peered into the basket. 'What's wrong with Tiddles?'

'Nothing,' Ernie said in his gruff voice.

'That's good,' Mandy said. 'Why are you bringing him in, then?'

'Injection,' Ernie said. He peered at Mandy's inquisitive face from under the old tweed flat-cap he often wore. 'Why aren't you at school, lass?'

'School holiday,' Mandy explained.

'Oh.' The old man shook his head. 'You youngsters have too many holidays nowadays.'

'Do we?' Mandy gave a huge sigh.

Ernie looked at her again. 'You don't sound as if you're enjoying yourself very much.'

'No, I'm not,' Mandy told him. 'In fact, Mr Bell, I'm having a horrible time.' To her embarrassment she found herself bursting into tears.

'Oh, dear.' Ernie fished a hanky from his pocket and handed it to her. 'Now, now, lass, don't cry. What on earth's the matter?'

'It's Lydia's rabbits,' Mandy sobbed. 'Oh, Mr Bell, we don't know what to do.'

'Lydia?' Ernie repeated. Everyone knew Ernie had a soft spot for her.

'Yes,' Mandy sniffed.

'Lydia's rabbits?' Ernie said. 'What's up with them, then?'

Between sniffs and sobs, Mandy told him.

By now they had reached the gate that led up the path to the surgery entrance. Ernie pushed it open and waited for Mandy to blow her nose. She offered the hanky back to him.

'No, no, you keep it, lass,' Ernie said hurriedly.

Mandy stuffed it into her pocket. 'Thank you, Mr Bell, I'm sorry. I've been trying to think how we might be able to save them but I can't think of a single thing.' Another tear ran down her cheek and she wiped it away impatiently.

Ernie looked thoughtful. Then he said, 'Look,

lass, why don't you go and see my old mate, Robbie Grimshaw?'

Mandy sniffed again and rubbed her face. 'Who's Robbie Grimshaw?'

'You mean you've never heard of him?'

She shook her head. 'No.'

'Well, I'll tell you something for nothing. There's not a thing about rabbits that Robbie doesn't know. If anyone'll be able to help you, he will.'

'But who *is* he?' Mandy asked again. 'Where does he live and how does he know all about rabbits?'

As they went through into the waiting-room Ernie explained. 'He lives by Lamb's Wood,' he told her. 'You go past Woodbridge Farm Park then turn up a little lane on the left. There's a bit of a smallholding along there . . . ramshackle old place.'

'Oh,' Mandy said. 'A bit like Lydia's.'

'A bit,' Ernie said. 'Good with creatures, Robbie is.' He gave a grin. 'And he used to be the bane of old Frank Western's life. Frank was Sam Western's father.'

'Why was that, then?' Mandy asked.

Ernie leaned his whiskery face close to hers. 'A gentleman of the night was Robbie,' he whispered, even though there was no one else in the waiting-room to hear him. Animal Ark's receptionist, Jean Knox, was using the photocopier in the back office.

Mandy frowned. 'Gentleman of the night?' she repeated, whispering too, although she didn't know why.

Ernie chuckled. 'Robbie was a poacher,' he explained. 'Best there was. Retired now, of course . . . Anyway, lass, you go and see him. He might have some ideas about those conies.'

'Right,' Mandy said eagerly. 'I will. Thanks for the suggestion, Mr Bell.'

'And give my regards to Lydia when you see her,' Ernie added as Mandy headed for the door.

'I will,' Mandy replied. 'We were planning to help her mend Houdini's shelter but we've been so worried about the rabbits we haven't got round to it yet.'

'Oh?' Ernie brightened. 'Well, tell Lydia I'd be pleased to take a look at it.'

'Oh, great, I will,' Mandy said, edging closer to the door. There wasn't any more time to talk now. She'd got to find out when James and John could go to see Robbie with her. He could be their only hope.

When she had said goodbye to Ernie, Mandy rushed straight over to James's house. He was clearing leaves from the Hunters' front garden. Blackie was having a great time, rolling in the piles of leaves and scattering them all over the place as soon as had James raked them up.

'Blackie! I'll tie you up,' he was threatening, as Mandy appeared at the gate.

Breathlessly she told him about Robbie.

James's eyes lit up. 'Great! By the time I've finished clearing up these leaves, John should be back from Walton. Then we can all go over and see this Robbie together.'

Mandy helped James put the leaves into bags, then they made their way along to the Fox and Goose. To their relief, John had just arrived back. As they told him about Robbie, his face lit up, but then he looked dubious when Mandy told him Robbie had been a poacher.

'That means he'll know about *killing* rabbits,' he said solemnly. 'Not *saving* them.'

Mandy bit her lip. 'I hadn't thought of that.'

'I think we should go and see him anyway,' James said. 'After all, Mr Bell said Robbie is retired now. And he's the only hope we've got at the moment.'

'I agree,' Mandy said determinedly. 'I don't care whether he was a poacher or not. He might be able to help us *save* our rabbits.'

John nodded. 'Well, I've been racking my brains and I can't think of anything,' he said. 'So let's go.'

They set off on their bikes. For once, Blackie was being good, trotting alongside James's bike and not pulling at his lead.

'Mr Bell told me there's not a thing Robbie doesn't know about rabbits,' Mandy told James and John, as they rode along the High Street and out on to the Walton road. 'So if he can't suggest anything, then no one else will be able to either.'

They went past the Farm Park and soon came to the narrow turning Mr Bell had described.

Stopping at the junction, they peered down the lane. It looked very neglected: a tunnel of overgrown trees that shut out the sky. NO THROUGH ROAD said a sign.

'Do you think we've come to the right place?' John asked doubtfully.

'This is where Mr Bell said,' Mandy assured him. 'Come on, let's go.' She pedalled on ahead.

The lane was uneven and bumpy. In places, grass had grown through the cracks in the old tarmac. It didn't look as if any vehicles had been along it for years.

Eventually it petered out and became a rough, unmade track.

'Are you *sure* this is right?' John said again. He looked worried as the branches overhead creaked and groaned in the brisk autumn wind. He glanced upward. 'It's a bit creepy.'

'Absolutely,' Mandy said, though she wasn't really sure herself now. Then suddenly a gate came into view. She sighed in relief. 'Look,' she pointed. 'There's a gate.'

LAMB'S WOOD COTTAGE said a rickety sign half hanging off the top bar. Beyond was what looked like a large wooden shack. But as they got closer they saw it was a weatherboarded cottage. It had once been painted white but now the surface was cracked and peeling, and green with moss. There was a muddy yard too, bordered by sheds and lean-tos even more tumbledown than Lydia's outbuildings. There was an old wagon to the side of one of the sheds and, stacked up nearby, a dozen or so shiny white ash sticks with their bark stripped off.

Hens, geese and ducks pecked and honked and waddled around the yard, and in a run-down old sty on the far side a sow and her litter slept in the shelter of the wall.

Mandy, James and John dumped their bikes and went through the gate, shutting it behind them. A couple of the geese ran hissing towards them, necks outstretched, wings flapping.

John took a step backwards, going quite pale. 'Oh!'

'It's OK.' Mandy sounded braver than she felt. 'I don't think they'll hurt you.'

To make matters worse, a black-and-white Welsh collie came bounding round from the

back of the house. It stood in front of them, hackles up, ears back. A deep growl came from its throat. Blackie stood still, tail wagging uncertainly. Slowly the dogs began sniffing round one another. Mandy held her breath. Blackie was always friendly with other dogs but she didn't think the collie was at all pleased to see him.

Then slowly the collie's tail began to wag as Blackie crouched with his bottom in the air, tail waving madly, ready for a game if the other dog wanted to play.

'Biddy . . . behave!' A gruff voice came from one of the sheds, and Mandy turned to see the strangest-looking figure she had ever seen emerging from the doorway. He was very short – hardly taller than Mandy herself. He wore baggy corduroy trousers, tied below the knee with orange baler twine. Above that was a long leather jerkin with a striped cotton shirt underneath, the sleeves rolled up to reveal sinewy brown arms. On his head was a tweed flat-cap, so old and battered it made Ernie Bell's look quite respectable. He had a grey beard and even from where she stood Mandy could see piercing blue eyes that narrowed as he frowned at her. He came towards them, and as he walked his legs bowed out and he rolled as if he was on board a ship.

'What can I do for you?' he called, looking suspicious.

Mandy swallowed nervously. Robbie Grimshaw might be a friend of Mr Bell's but he looked ten times as grumpy and not one bit pleased to see them.

'Um,' she swallowed again. 'Ernie Bell told us you might be able to help us.' By now, Biddy and Blackie were scampering round the farmyard, growling at each other and pretending to scrap.

'Ernie, aye?' Robbie said. He relaxed a little as he recognised the name. 'Well . . . what *do* you want?' He still looked grumpy and out of sorts.

Mandy decided to take the bull by the horns. She went forward and held out her hand. 'I'm Mandy Hope, the local vets' daughter, and these are my friends: James Hunter and John Hardy.'

'Vets?' Robbie frowned. 'What vets?'

'Adam and Emily Hope,' Mandy said.

'Oh,' Robbie said. 'Them vets. Met your father once when my Kirsty was sick.'

Close up, Mandy could see Robbie's face was brown and wrinkled as a nut, and the hand he held out to shake hers was bent and gnarled, like the bark of an oak tree.

'Mandy, James and John.' The old man's eyes twinkled and Mandy gave a quiet sigh of relief. It looked as if Robbie was a bit like his pal, Ernie. All gruff and grumpy on the outside but nice once he got to know you.

'Well,' Robbie went on. 'What can I do for you?'

When they told him their problem, he stroked his beard and looked thoughtful. He was taking so long to comment, Mandy thought he wasn't going to say anything at all.

Eventually, though, he spoke. 'Lydia Fawcett, eh?' he said. His eyes twinkled again. 'Is she still bonny?'

Mandy didn't think 'bonny' was *exactly* the right word to describe no-nonsense Lydia, even though she knew that was what Ernie Bell thought she was.

'Er . . . well,' she said. 'She's very *nice*.'

'Aye, she always was very nice,' Robbie said in a faraway voice.

'But what about the rabbits?' James blurted out. 'And Mr Western?'

'Sam Western,' Robbie said thoughtfully. 'Had a lot of dealings with old Frank Western, his father.'

'Did you?' Mandy asked.

'Aye, pretty crafty he was,' Robbie said, grinning. 'But not as crafty as me. Mind you,' he went on, 'he did nab me once or twice with a few of his conies slung over my back.'

'Conies?' John asked, frowning.

'Aye . . . rabbits to you, lad.' Robbie chuckled. 'Had the constable lock me up for the night, on one occasion. But I'll say this for old Frank: he never took me to court.'

James gazed at Robbie with wide eyes. 'So you really were a poacher?' he breathed.

Robbie winked one eye solemnly at James. 'I might have been,' he said. 'Then again, I might not.' Robbie seemed to be talking in riddles.

'So will you help us, then?' John asked impatiently. 'Only we need to know, and Lydia will want to know too, when she hears that we've been to see you. She's as worried about the rabbits as we are.'

Robbie looked thoughtful again. 'I reckon I'd better come up and see this flick o' rabbits,' he said. 'Cast my eye over 'em . . . See if I think anything *can* be done.'

'This *what* of rabbits?' James asked, looking puzzled.

'Flick,' Robbie replied. 'It's what you call a colony of 'em. Flick or kindle, it don't matter which. Or if you want to call them conies, it's a game.'

Now they all looked bewildered. 'A *game*?' Mandy asked. Robbie seemed to be talking in riddles again.

'Aye, a game of conies.' Robbie confirmed. 'Lovely creatures . . . especially in a pie with home-grown potatoes and cabbage.'

Mandy's heart sank. Perhaps John had been right. Maybe Robbie Grimshaw *did* only care

about killing rabbits for food. Maybe they were
wasting their time.

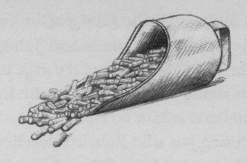

Five

Robbie must have seen Mandy's worried expression because he suddenly laughed, a deep rumble that came right up from his stomach and echoed round the yard. 'I'm only teasing, lass. I don't go killing conies for trade these days. I prefer just to watch them.'

He scratched his head then turned to look behind him at one of the tumbledown old sheds, then said, 'Look, why don't you all come and have a look round?' He grinned at Mandy. 'If you're the vets' lass you'll like my animals. Come and watch me feed my lovelies, then we'll go and see Lydia. All right?'

Mandy beamed at James and John. 'That sounds brilliant!' She resisted the urge to throw her arms round Robbie. She had the feeling it would embarrass him no end.

Wondering just who Robbie's 'lovelies' were, Mandy, James and John followed him into one of the old sheds. Straight away they saw who he meant. In cages ranged along the wall were three bright-eyed ferrets.

Mandy drew in her breath. 'Oh, Mr Grimshaw, I *love* ferrets! May I help you feed them?'

'Course you can,' the old man replied. He opened an old dustbin and took out a scoopful of dried food. 'They'll be pleased to meet you, I'm sure.'

The ferret cages were large, light and airy. Inside, Robbie had put lengths of pipe so they could run in and out. Mandy knew that ferrets were members of the polecat family which lived in burrows and tunnels in the wild.

Robbie's little creatures were standing up against the wire, waiting for their meal. They had long, slender, furry bodies, long tails, short legs and dainty, clawed feet. Mandy thought their bright eyes, delicate pointed noses and soft coats looked adorable. But she knew ferrets *could* give you a nasty bite if they were frightened, so she waited while Robbie undid the hooks on the cages.

'Their teeth look pretty sharp.' John sounded wary as he peered at them over Mandy's shoulder. 'I saw one on TV. It sank its teeth into a man's finger and wouldn't let go.'

Robbie chuckled. 'Aye, they can be a bit like that. But not my lovelies. I've had them since they were kits and they're gentle as lambs.'

'This is Kirsty.' He undid the catch on the first cage. 'She's a jill.' The honey-coloured ferret with pink eyes and nose made a little noise of greeting in her throat.

'A jill?' John looked confused. 'I thought you said her name was Kirsty?'

Mandy laughed. 'Female ferrets are called jills, aren't they, Mr Grimshaw?'

'Quite right.' Robbie put his hand into the cage and gently scooped the ferret out.

'Are males called jacks?' James asked. 'You know . . . Jack and Jill . . .'

Robbie chuckled and shook his head. 'No, they're called hobs.' He held the ferret out towards John. 'Here, lad, take her. She won't hurt you.'

'Er . . . no, it's all right, thanks.' John took a step back, still not sure whether he could trust the little creature not to bite him.

But Mandy held out her hands eagerly and took Kirsty into her arms. The ferret looked at her, gazing with bright, pink eyes as if she was trying to work out what Mandy was thinking. Her tiny nose sniffed the air. Mandy stroked her head and felt the delicate bones under her fingers. Kirsty's fur was soft and fine and her body felt lithe and sensitive.

'Oh!' Mandy breathed. She looked at the old man, her eyes shining. 'She's gorgeous.'

'Told you,' Robbie smiled proudly. He introduced them to the others. 'This is Marlon.' He opened the second cage and took out a dark brown, almost black ferret. 'He smells a bit,' Robbie told them. 'Ferrets do. But I don't mind, do I, boy?' He stroked the ferret affectionately, then let it run up his arm and weave itself round his neck like a fur scarf. Mandy couldn't help giggling as the little creature peeped out from behind Robbie's cap with eyes like dark beads.

Finally, Robbie took out the third ferret, another brownish-black. 'This is Sable,' he told Mandy. 'She's a beauty. Here . . .' He held Sable towards John. 'Take her.'

This time John took the ferret warily into his arms and held her gently. He relaxed as he stroked her soft fur, then looked at Robbie with

shining eyes. 'She's great,' he said.

Mandy stood spellbound as Kirsty climbed up on to her shoulders. 'She's so lovely.' She rubbed her cheek against the ferret's soft fur. 'Are they your favourite pets, Mr Grimshaw?'

'Pets?' Robbie said. Then he sighed. 'Oh, aye, I suppose they are. They're really working animals, but they don't do much of that nowadays.'

They listened intently as Robbie explained how ferrets could be used in rabbit-hunting. They were put down rabbit holes to flush them out. He told them how rabbits were then caught in purse nets that had been pegged out round the entrance to their burrows. When they ran out of their holes to escape from the ferrets they ran straight into the nets. Then the hunter pulled up a drawstring and the rabbits were trapped.

'Don't the ferrets kill them?' John asked anxiously.

'Oh, aye, sometimes,' Robbie told him. 'Sometimes they need to be muzzled. If they catch a rabbit they eat it then fall asleep down in the warren. They "hole up" as we call it.'

'Oh,' Mandy said. 'What happens then?'

'Well, sometimes you have to dig them out, but if you can't locate them you just have to keep going back and hope to find them.'

Robbie must have seen Mandy looked worried about this, because he patted her on the shoulder. 'But don't you worry. If it's saving rabbits you want, then that's what we'll try to do.' He put Marlon back in his cage and took the others from Mandy and John. He picked up the scoop of food and handed it to Mandy to fill the ferrets' bowls. 'There you are, my beauties,' he cooed. 'Right,' he went on. 'I'll just get my trusty steed and we'll be on our way to Lydia's.'

Mandy wondered what his trusty steed was. Maybe Robbie had a horse or a pony out in the field that he would ride up to High Cross.

Robbie came back with the most rusty old bicycle they had ever seen. For a minute Mandy thought she had misheard Robbie and that he had said *rusty* steed, not *trusty* steed.

'You're not going to ride *that*, are you?' James asked incredulously.

Robbie swung his leg over the tatty saddle. 'Nothing wrong with this, my lad,' he said. 'Over sixty years old this bike and it's as good as new.'

'But it hasn't got any gears!' Mandy could hardly believe the old man wasn't joking.

'Gears?' he called as he pedalled off, with Biddy barking by his side. 'Who needs gears?' Blackie followed Biddy excitedly.

'Stay, Biddy!' Robbie commanded the collie, and she slunk back into the yard leaving Blackie to wait for the others to catch up.

Giggling, Mandy, James and John got on their bikes and pedalled after Robbie.

'I used to do all my . . . er . . . night work on this bike,' Robbie called over his shoulder as he rode jauntily down the lane towards the junction with the Walton road. The bike rattled over the potholes and squeaked merrily with every turn of the wheels.

'But it hasn't got any lights,' John remarked.

'Lights?' Robbie exclaimed. 'I didn't need lights, lad. All I needed was the light of the moon. Besides, if you had lights, gamekeepers could spot you a mile off.'

'Couldn't they *hear* you?' John asked. 'That bike makes enough noise to wake the dead.'

'Oh, she didn't squeak at all in those days,' Robbie assured him. 'And you had to go out on windy nights, you know. Sound travels too much on still nights.'

'I bet,' James said. 'But you did get caught sometimes. You told us.'

'Oh, aye,' Robbie panted a little as they rode up the hill that led to High Cross. 'Sometimes.'

'It must have been pretty exciting,' James said.

Robbie threw him a glance. 'Oh, aye, I suppose it was. But it was the only way I could get food for my family in the wintertime, lad. So don't you think I did it for sport, will you?'

'Oh, no,' James said hastily, although Robbie gave him such a huge wink Mandy wasn't at all sure he was telling the whole truth.

At High Cross, Lydia was in the kitchen as they came through the gate. Robbie put his feet down and brought the bicycle to a halt. It not only didn't have lights, it didn't have any brakes either. Mandy couldn't stifle a giggle as the toe-caps of Robbie's old leather boots scuffed up a storm of dust.

Lydia opened the door to greet them and looked in surprise at Robbie. 'Well,' she said. 'Robbie Grimshaw! I haven't seen you for years, you old scallywag. What are you doing here?'

Robbie doffed his cap and grinned at her. 'Lydia Fawcett,' he said. 'Still as bonny as ever.'

'Get away with you,' Lydia said as she stepped aside to let them in. Mandy wasn't sure but she thought she saw Lydia blush. 'Come in, all of you.'

'We used to see each other at the village hall dances,' Robbie whispered to Mandy as they went in.

'Oh,' Mandy said. Somehow she couldn't imagine Robbie and Lydia taking a turn round the floor.

Lydia overheard what Robbie had said. 'That was years ago,' she said. 'When they used to have dances every week.'

They sat in the kitchen while Robbie told Lydia the reason for his visit.

When it seemed he had finished, John piped up impatiently, 'Can we show you the rabbits now?'

'Right, then.' Robbie winked at Lydia. 'Lead the way.'

They went outside. Lydia walked behind with Robbie as they all made their way across the goat paddock. At the stile they stopped, looking out towards Sam Western's land. Mandy was alarmed to see more maize kernels lying on the ground and the rabbits running in and out of Sam Western's field.

'Oh, no,' John exclaimed. 'They're still at it.'

'Aye, they would be,' Robbie said wisely. 'One of their favourite foods, corncobs. Nice and sweet, you see.'

Mandy spotted the big rabbit again. He was by the warren, balancing on a tree root, ears pricked. Again she was sure he was their leader. He looked so alert, his nose sniffing the wind for danger.

Then he must have smelled a human because suddenly he seemed to freeze. Only his nose moved, nostrils flaring. He stamped his back legs as a danger signal and with a vivid white tail-flick he bolted down the nearest hole. The others followed, spreading out, scattering, a whole storm of running, hopping, white bob-tails, until, with one last flick of powerful hind legs, there were no rabbits left to be seen.

Mandy turned to Robbie, her eyes shining. 'Did you see them? Aren't they brilliant?'

'Aye, I saw them,' Robbie confirmed. 'And I saw Sam Western's corn in their sharp little teeth.' He rubbed his beard and shook his head. 'He's right, you know, something's got to be done.'

'We know that.' Mandy could see John was getting agitated again. 'And we've got to do it before Monday.'

Robbie clambered over the stile and they all followed, walking the boundary of Lydia's land. Robbie looked deep in thought, rolling along with his hands behind his back. At last he said, 'Well, there's two ways of keeping 'em on this side of the boundary that spring to mind.'

'What are they?' Mandy asked eagerly.

'Well, you could think about erecting a tall

fence along the boundary to Western's land,'
Robbie replied. 'But an ordinary sheep-wire
fence wouldn't be any good. You see, rabbits
can dig under the mesh, or even climb over, if
they set their mind to it,' he explained. 'You'd
need to dig a trench right round the boundary,
sink a fence into it then fill the trench with
water.'

Lydia looked at him in horror. 'I couldn't even
afford to have an ordinary fence built. What
you've just described would cost a fortune –
never mind that it would take weeks to build!'

'And we've only got till Sunday night,' John
wailed.

'True,' Robbie stroked his beard.

'But there must be *some* kind of rabbit-proof
fence we could put up quickly and cheaply,'
Mandy insisted.

Robbie looked doubtful, then continued.
'Let's see now. If you couldn't manage the
trench fence, then one with a fifteen-centimetre
ledge on this side, top and bottom, would do as
well.'

'How does that work, then?' James asked.

'Well,' Robbie explained. 'A coney's first instinct when it comes up to an object is to burrow underneath it. But it won't do this if it finds fencing under its front paws rather than earth. The same at the top; if he finds a ledge he won't try to get over it.'

Lydia was shaking her head sadly. 'It's no good, Robbie. It's all too expensive, and even if it wasn't we'd never get fences like that put up in time.'

Suddenly, Mandy had an idea. 'Mr Bell!' she blurted out.

'Ernie Bell?' Robbie frowned at her. 'What about him?'

'He was a carpenter. He'd make the fence, I'm sure,' Mandy said. She turned to Lydia. 'He's already said he'll come and see to Houdini's shelter.'

'Yes, he would, honestly,' James insisted before Lydia could comment. 'Let's measure up—'

But Lydia held up her hand. 'It's no good, you two. Even if there was an army of carpenters I couldn't afford it. I'm sorry.'

'Oh,' Mandy said in a small voice. She felt so crestfallen she could have cried. It would be all right if they had the time and the money. But they hadn't got either. Her heart sank. Saving the rabbits was looking more and more hopeless.

They all stared at Robbie. *Please think of something*, Mandy prayed. *Surely there must be some other solution?*

But Robbie was shaking his head. 'I'm sorry,' he said. 'But, apart from building a rabbit-proof fence or shooting them, there's absolutely nothing else anyone can do to stop those little varmints eating that corn.'

John looked as if he was about to burst into tears. Mandy put her arm round him. 'We'll think of something, honestly we will.' She sounded a lot more confident that she felt.

As the dejected party made their way back to Lydia's house, Mandy wished she really *could* think of something. She was racking her brains like mad but wasn't coming up with a single thing.

'Come in and have a drink and a biscuit,

everyone,' Lydia suggested. 'It might make us feel a bit better.'

But as they sat round Lydia's table Mandy knew it would take a lot more than a glass of lemonade and one of Lydia's home-made biscuits to cheer them up.

'Well . . .' Robbie looked round at their forlorn faces. 'Unless we can think of something, I'm very much afraid Sunday looks like the end of the line for your conies.'

Six

'You've got a long face,' Simon said to Mandy when she arrived back at Animal Ark. It was mid-afternoon and she had chores to do before evening surgery. Both Mr and Mrs Hope were out on calls.

John had gone home with James, and Robbie had been invited to stay on at Lydia's while she showed him her goats and took him on a tour of her farm.

They had cycled back from High Cross with heavy hearts. It really looked as if their battle to save the rabbits was lost.

Mandy sighed. 'Yes, I know,' she said in reply to Simon's comment. 'It's because I'm really worried.'

Simon hitched himself up on to the examination table. 'OK,' he said gently. 'Tell me – what are you so worried about?'

Mandy explained as she fetched a bowl of hot water and disinfectant and a cloth to wipe down the work surfaces. She banged the bowl down so hard the water splashed down the front of her jeans. '. . . And I can't bear the thought of those poor rabbits getting shot,' she finished angrily.

Simon gave a sigh. 'You can't always win your battles, Mandy. Sometimes you've got to give in gracefully.'

'I know, that's the problem.' Mandy said stubbornly. 'I *can't* give in gracefully when animals are going to be killed. And anyway, I won't.'

Just then Jean put her head round the door. 'There's someone here who can't wait until evening surgery, Simon. Could you see her?'

Simon smiled. 'Show her through. I'll do what

I can, but she might need to see Adam or Emily later.'

Jean nodded and turned to someone standing behind her. 'Would you like to come through?'

A girl of about seventeen with long dark hair and brown eyes came in to the room. She was dressed in jeans and a check shirt and carried a large cardboard box in her arms. She introduced herself as Jo Entwistle.

Mandy recognised her. Her family had recently moved into The Cedars, a large house on the Walton road. Mandy's friend, Susan Collins, lived at The Beeches nearby, and Mandy had seen the girl when she'd visited. The newcomers had two lively Jack Russell terriers and had been at The Cedars for about three months.

'What have you got there?' Simon eyed the box.

'A cat,' she replied. 'He's just turned up at our house,' she explained, as she opened the box. Inside was a grey cat with enormous greeny-blue eyes. Its coat was matted and tangled and it looked half starved. One ear was scarred and torn where it had been in a fight. It looked out at Simon and gave a thin miaow.

Mandy's hand flew to her mouth. She recognised the cat by his torn ear. His name was Georgie and he had belonged to Mr and Mrs Wilson, the people who used to live at The Cedars.

'It's Georgie!' She looked at Simon with tears in her eyes. 'What happened to him? And what on earth is he doing back in Welford?'

'We recognised him too,' Jo told them. 'The previous owners of our house, Mr and Mrs

Wilson, phoned weeks ago to say he'd gone missing,' she explained. 'And we'd seen him briefly once before, when we came to view the house before we bought it.' Jo looked at the poor bedraggled creature and shook her head. 'But we never dreamed he'd really turn up back here. We've just found him at our back door.'

'But the Wilsons moved *miles* away!' Mandy was hardly able to believe what she was hearing.

'I know,' Jo answered with a shrug. 'Goodness knows how he got here.'

'He walked.' Simon was examining Georgie's paws. 'Look how sore his feet are.'

'Oh, poor thing,' Mandy murmured.

'We can't have him at home because of the terriers,' Jo told them.

'Well, I can't see anything that a few good meals won't put right,' Simon said, as he examined Georgie. 'But Mr or Mrs Hope will need to check him over. I'm sure they'll be happy to treat him until the Wilsons can fetch him, as long as it's only for a few days.'

Jo smiled. 'That's great. I've already phoned Mrs Wilson and she said they'll come as soon as they can.' She fished a bit of paper from the back pocket of her jeans. 'And here's the Wilsons' number. Could you ring them and tell them how he's getting on, please?'

'Yes, of course we will.' Mandy took the paper from her. 'And thanks,' she called as Jo left.

Georgie was still crouched on the table, hardly able to put his sore feet down, when Mrs Hope arrived back. She put down her bag and came to take a look at the cat.

'Surely he couldn't have come all that way by himself,' Mandy said. She still could hardly believe it.

'Cats do.' Emily Hope agreed with Simon that, apart from his sore feet and loss of weight, Georgie seemed none the worse for his ordeal.

Mandy watched as Simon gently bathed Georgie's feet and covered them with soothing antiseptic ointment.

'I'll give him a shot of antibiotic in case there's any infection,' Mrs Hope said to Simon when he'd finished. Simon went to prepare the syringe. 'It's not unknown for cats to walk much further than Georgie has,' she told Mandy.

'They sometimes turn up years later.'

'But how do they know the way?' Mandy asked incredulously.

Her mum shrugged. 'No one really knows. You see cats aren't like dogs. Dogs are happy simply to be with their masters, but cats don't like moving house.'

'I see.' Mandy held Georgie gently as Mrs Hope gave him his shot. She rubbed the loose skin at the back of his neck where the needle went in.

'People don't always realise you should keep a cat indoors in a new house for a few weeks,' Mrs Hope explained. 'Then you should only let them out when they're hungry. Once they know where their food and shelter is everything should be OK. Mr and Mrs Wilson obviously didn't know that.'

'Well, I think it's a miracle,' Mandy said. She stroked Georgie. 'You're a very clever puss.'

Her mum smiled. 'Yes, he is.' She gently handed him to Simon. 'He's ready for the residential unit now. And I think a small meal, don't you?'

'I'll get it,' Mandy said eagerly.

'Not too much now,' Mrs Hope told her. 'He's obviously half starved, so just a little at a time until his stomach is more able to cope.'

'Right.' Mandy went into the food store and brought out a tin of cat food. She opened it, spooned a little into a dish then took it through to Georgie.

The cat was curled up on a soft blanket in his wire cage, already looking a lot happier than when he'd arrived. He lifted his head eagerly as he smelled the food coming his way. Soon he was gobbling it up as if his life depended upon it. Mandy stroked his head.

'Didn't you like your new home?' she asked him. She thought how she would hate to move away from Welford. She couldn't imagine a nicer place to live.

Then, suddenly, an idea hit her like a bombshell: did *rabbits* mind moving to a new home? If they didn't then maybe that was the answer. If Lydia's rabbits could live somewhere else then their problem would be solved.

But what if they didn't like being moved?

What if they went back to their old home?

There was only one thing to do: ask Robbie tomorrow.

Mandy quickly closed the cage door. She must tell James and John, and Lydia.

She hurried to the phone and called James's number. 'Come on, come on,' she said impatiently, as she waited for someone to answer. Finally James himself picked up the phone. 'Hey!' Mandy breathed, 'I've just had the most brilliant idea . . .'

When Mandy had finished explaining, James agreed her idea did sound brilliant.

John was still there, and he agreed too. 'First thing tomorrow, we'll go and see what Robbie thinks of it,' he said, excitedly.

Mandy then phoned Lydia to tell her about her idea.

'It might work,' Lydia said thoughtfully. 'I'm sure Robbie will know.'

'We're going to see him about it first thing in the morning,' Mandy told her.

'First thing?' Lydia said. 'Oh, Robbie's coming here. I told him tomorrow was my baking day, and he invited himself round,' Lydia said, laughing.

'We'll come to High Cross, then,' Mandy said. 'If that's all right.'

'Of course it is,' Lydia confirmed. 'I'll look forward to seeing you.'

The next morning, James and John were waiting at the village green for Mandy, excited as she was about the possible solution to their problems.

They hurried on their way. If Robbie thought relocating the rabbits was a good idea they could get started on a plan to save them.

Robbie's bike was propped up against the fence as they arrived at High Cross. Lydia had opened the front door before they had the chance to knock.

Robbie was sitting at the kitchen table drinking a mug of tea. He listened carefully as Mandy told him her scheme.

'If we could catch all the rabbits and take them somewhere else,' she suggested eagerly, 'somewhere a long way away from Mr Western's crops, then he'll have nothing more to moan about, will he?'

'I think it's a brilliant idea!' John's eyes were shining. He turned to Robbie. 'It would work, wouldn't it?'

But Robbie looked doubtful. 'I don't know if we could do that.'

'Why not,' Mandy demanded to know. Then her face fell. 'Oh . . . they'd come back, would they? Like cats sometimes do?'

Robbie shook his head. 'No, probably not. Rabbits don't have particularly strong homing instincts, and don't travel long distances. They need to be able to run home quickly if they're threatened. So as long as their new location provides what they need, they'd be likely to settle.'

'So what kind of place would we need to look for?' James asked.

Robbie scratched his chin. 'Let's see now . . . Basically conies need cover and food. Brambles, gorse, shrubs, trees – perhaps a small piece of woodland – with sandy, free-draining soil for them to burrow under.'

'Well, I'm sure we could manage that,' Mandy said. 'We could at least have a go!' She looked at Robbie pleadingly.

'Well . . . I've never heard of such a thing before,' he said, shaking his head.

'But it *could* just work, couldn't it?' James asked, staring at Robbie.

The old man bit his lip. 'I suppose we could try—'

Mandy wanted to jump for joy. 'Oh, Robbie, it would be great!'

'But you'd have to catch 'em first,' he said. 'That wouldn't be easy . . . not that many.'

'So we'd need bait of some kind?' Mandy asked.

Robbie nodded. 'Aye, carrots would do. Or corncobs, we *know* they like those.' Robbie was clearly warming to the idea.

Lydia held up her hand. 'Hold on, you four, you're getting carried away. Even if we *did* manage to catch all the rabbits, where could we take them?'

Robbie scratched his chin.

'Do you know anywhere like you described earlier?' James asked.

'Lots of places,' Robbie replied. 'But most of them have got rabbits there already. They wouldn't take kindly to a new flick turning up in their territory.'

'Then we've got to find somewhere that *hasn't* already got rabbits,' John said matter of factly.

This time Mandy held up her hand. She was getting a bit lost in all the suggestions flying around. 'Let's write it all down,' she said. 'Then maybe we can get something organised.'

They sat down at the table as Lydia brought a pencil and note-pad. Mandy took the pencil and sucked the end thoughtfully. Then she wrote: *Operation Rabbits on the Run.*

'Right, everybody,' she said. 'First, Robbie needs to decide the best way to catch them.'

Robbie chewed the edge of his thumbnail thoughtfully. 'As there's so many of them we couldn't use live capture cages but we *could* do what we used to call long netting.'

John stared at him. 'What's that?'

Robbie explained. 'We used to make long nets

that we'd peg out all round the warren on tall sticks. Then we'd leave it overnight. The rabbits wouldn't see the nets in the dark and blunder into them, get caught up and we'd go back and collect them in the morning. Easy.'

'Sounds a brilliant idea,' James said.

'Hmm,' Robbie stroked his beard. 'Trouble was, they struggled so much to get free they often broke their legs, or necks . . . I don't really think that would do.'

'No, definitely not,' Mandy agreed. 'We don't want any of them getting injured.'

'What then?' John piped up.

Mandy gazed at Robbie, waiting for another suggestion. He raised his eyebrows then said, 'How about using my ferrets?'

Mandy went on staring at him, open-mouthed. Kirsty, Marlon and Sable! *Of course!* 'You mean using them with purse nets like you told us about?' she asked.

Robbie nodded. 'That's right, lass.'

'But where could we get the nets?' she asked.

Robbie gave her a wink. 'Oh, I reckon I've got enough stored away somewhere.'

'Yes, I bet you have.' Lydia tried to look stern but only managed a smile instead.

'And we don't want any of them to get killed,' John said anxiously.

'Don't worry,' Robbie assured him. 'I've got some ferret muzzles too.'

'That's absolutely great.' Mandy sat back. She had a sudden soaring feeling everything was going to be all right after all. Until she thought of another problem and came back down to earth with a bump. She bit her lip. 'We can't carry them in the nets, though, can we?' she asked, gazing at Robbie with a worried expression on her face.

Robbie shook his head. 'No, what we really need to carry them in is dark cotton bags – the darkness would stop them from panicking.'

'Dark cotton bags?' James repeated. 'Where could we get them?'

'My gran could make them on her sewing machine,' Mandy volunteered.

'We'd need loads,' James said. 'She'd never do it in time.'

'Boxes,' Lydia said suddenly. 'We could put

them in cardboard boxes. Couldn't we, Robbie?'

'Oh, aye,' Robbie said. 'Boxes would be fine. As long as they're in the dark while they're being transported, they won't panic.'

'Right,' Lydia said. 'When I take my delivery of milk to the supermarket in Walton tomorrow, I'll get some grocery boxes. There's always lots stacked outside. How about that, then?'

'Oh, Lydia, that would be brilliant,' Mandy cried.

'We'll need help catching 'em,' Robbie went on. 'We can't do it on our own . . . too many rabbits, not enough time.'

'Mum and Dad will lend us a hand.' Mandy said confidently. She sat down again and wrote *cardboard boxes* on her list. Then she began a list of names. 'And Gran and Grandad. And Simon . . .'

'And so will my dad,' John said. 'And Sara – I'm sure she'll help, too.'

'And my mum and dad,' James added.

'Now,' Robbie said, bringing them all back to earth with a bump. 'Most important of all, *where* are we going to take them?'

There was silence as everybody tried to think of somewhere.

'Monkton Spinney?' James suggested hopefully.

Robbie shook his head. 'No good,' he said. 'It's overrun with conies already.'

'Oh,' James looked crestfallen.

'How about Mrs Janeki's?' Mandy volunteered. Dora Janeki was a sheep farmer who lived at Syke Farm, a mile or so away.

But Lydia shook her head. 'She doesn't like rabbits any more than Sam Western, I don't suppose,' she said. 'It's got to be somewhere where they can't be a nuisance to anyone.'

'Far away from any farms,' Robbie said. 'Especially Sam Western's.'

Mandy's pencil hovered over the page. 'I can't think of anywhere,' she said in a small voice.

Robbie frowned. 'Of course, what would be ideal is a warren that has been abandoned by a previous colony. Our rabbits could then just take it over. Otherwise, we'd need to encourage them to start one by digging the first few holes.'

'Why might a rabbit colony abandon their warren?' James asked curiously.

Robbie shrugged. 'Lots of reasons. Too many foxes in the area, perhaps. Too many people. Sometimes the warrens get flooded in heavy rain, and the rabbits move on.'

'And sometimes they all get shot,' John added.

They all sat with their elbows on the table, staring at one another.

Mandy suddenly shut the note-pad with a loud thud. 'We'll have to go and look,' she said. They had got this far and they weren't going to be beaten now. She got up. 'Sitting here thinking about it isn't helping at all. We've got to go out and *find* somewhere.'

The others got to their feet. 'I'll come with you,' Robbie said.

Lydia came out with them. 'Ring me later,' she said to Mandy. 'And let me know how you get on.'

'I will,' Mandy called as they cycled off.

'Where do we start?' James asked when they reached the end of Lydia's drive.

'We'll go up to the Beacon,' Robbie said. 'I haven't been up there for some time. There used to be lots of rabbits up there years ago, but now . . . well, let's go and see.'

There *were* lots of places on the Beacon suitable for rabbits. Long banks and ridges where crooked hawthorns grew. One or two small, windblown spinneys. Past the Celtic cross and down the other side there was a wooded valley with a stream. But the trouble was, there were colonies of rabbits there already. They could see them from the footpath long before the animals spotted them coming and dived down into their burrows.

Robbie shook his head. 'No good,' he said. 'It'll have to be somewhere else.'

'We could ask Mr Marsh at Woodbridge Farm,' Mandy suggested. 'He might know of somewhere.'

Robbie shook his head. 'He's got two or three warrens on his land. I thinned them out for him last year. They were becoming a bit of a pest.'

'Oh, dear,' Mandy commented.

'Sorry, lass,' Robbie looked at her. 'But it had to be done. Better than getting rid of them all as Sam Western intends to do.'

She sighed. 'Yes, I suppose so.'

'There's nowhere near your house where we could take them, is there?' James asked Robbie. 'That big wood at the back?'

'Lamb's Wood?' Robbie shook his head. 'Overrun with 'em already, lad.'

They rode slowly along the road as far as the stone bridge across the river. After their first rush from High Cross they'd had to slow down as Robbie kept getting left behind. On the bridge, they stopped to wait for him to catch up again. Water bubbled over the rocks beneath. In the distance, the moorland rolled away in a haze of purple and green.

'We could look up there,' John said, looking out across the moor.

Robbie had caught them up. He shook his head. 'Ground's too hard,' he said. 'And besides there's no cover for them. Sparrowhawks and buzzards are fond of baby rabbits. It wouldn't do at all.'

'Well, then, if you ask me, we're banging our heads against a brick wall.' John sounded angry and frustrated. 'We've just been wasting our time.'

With that he turned and pedalled off back towards the village. The others stared after him in dismay.

'It's because he can't bear to think about them being killed,' James told Robbie. 'He really loves rabbits, you see.' He turned to Mandy. 'Come on, Mandy, we'd better go after him.'

'Aye and I'd better get back to see to my animals,' Robbie said. 'I'll let you know if I think of anywhere. If not, we'll carry on looking tomorrow.'

'Thanks, Robbie.' Mandy felt dejected. 'But we'll have to hurry up. Time's running out.'

Seven

When Mandy and James reached the Fox and Goose, Sara and Julian Hardy had just arrived back from Walton.

'I thought you three had gone out together?' John's stepmother looked surprised when she saw Mandy and James riding towards her without him.

Mandy explained. 'He's really upset,' she added.

'Oh dear,' Sara bit her lip. 'He was so excited this morning because we were going to collect his first batch of photos. I hope this doesn't spoil it for him.'

'I thought he could do his own developing,' Mandy said. She remembered John had set up his own darkroom in his bathroom during the summer holidays.

Julian nodded. 'John can develop his own black-and-white films,' he explained. 'But developing a colour film is far too complicated. So it has to go to a laboratory.'

'Oh,' Mandy said. 'I see.'

They left Julian unloading shopping from the boot of the car and followed Sara round the back of the pub and through the kitchen door.

They found John upstairs, sitting in front of the television. He looked surprised and a bit sheepish when they all trooped in.

'Sorry,' he said. 'I didn't mean to go off in a temper.'

Mandy went and sat on the sofa beside him. She knew how he felt. But it wouldn't do any good feeling angry and upset. They had to keep searching for somewhere they could move the rabbits to. They couldn't simply give up. 'It's OK,' she assured him. 'It doesn't matter.'

Sara handed John his photos with a smile.

'Maybe these will cheer you up, John,' she said. 'The man in the photography shop said they were really good.'

The photos *were* really good. There were some of the rabbits at High Cross. John had zoomed in on the one Mandy thought of as the king. He looked magnificent with the sun shining behind him as he sat combing his ears.

'That one's brilliant!' Mandy exclaimed.

John passed it to her and she stared at it, swallowing a lump that came into her throat. How could anyone think of killing such a lovely wild creature?

James and John thumbed through the others. Sara stood looking over their shoulder. 'Where's this?' She picked up one John had taken at Longstone Edge.

Mandy explained. 'It's lovely up there. So quiet.'

'It looks gorgeous.' Sara handed the picture to her.

Mandy stared at it for a moment or two. She was just going to hand it back to John when she suddenly stopped. She frowned and peered closer. The picture was of the clearing, brambles and tree stumps all around. The deep ruts made by the wheels of the foresters' machine were in the foreground. And there, beneath the brambles, was something she hadn't noticed before. Rabbit holes.

She looked at James and John. 'Did you see any rabbits when we were up there?'

They both shook their heads.

'Blackie was charging around looking for them,' James told her. 'But I don't think he even got a sniff of one.'

'If they've been coppicing up there maybe the tractors and chainsaws have driven them away,' Sara suggested.

'Yes.' Mandy's eyes began to shine. 'That's right, and if they have gone they'll have left an empty warren that might be just right for *our* rabbits.'

John stared at her, open-mouthed. 'Mandy, that would be brilliant!'

James looked from one to the other. 'They might not have gone,' he said, cautiously. 'They might just have heard us and were keeping well out of the way.'

'Well, there's only one thing for it,' Mandy said. 'We'll have to fetch Robbie and go and find out.' She jumped up. 'Come on, you two.'

'Right.' John put the photos back in their folder and put it in his pocket. 'Let's go.'

'But—?' Sara began. 'You haven't had any lunch.'

'I'll have something later,' John called. 'We won't be long,' he shouted as they clattered down the stairs, ran outside and grabbed their bikes.

As they raced along the Walton road towards the lane that led to Lamb's Wood Cottage, Mandy's heart was singing. They might have found a new home for the rabbits. All they needed was Robbie's confirmation, help from friends and family and Operation Rabbits on the Run could be well under way!

They arrived at Robbie's, red in the face and out of breath. He was sitting in the shelter of the barn, sorting out a boxful of dusty purse nets.

In the old lean-to, Kirsty, Marlon and Sable

were curled up in their cages, fast asleep, and in the sty, the sow and her piglets were gobbling food out of their trough. Biddy was sitting by Robbie's feet. She bounded over to them, tail wagging as they hurtled into the yard.

Robbie looked up, surprised to see them again so soon. 'My goodness, you three, what's happened now?' he called

They parked their bikes and ran across.

John dragged the photos from his pocket. 'Look, Robbie!'

Robbie fumbled in his inside pocket and took out a battered spectacle case. He opened it and put them on, peering at the photos as if he couldn't really see any better at all.

'That's Longstone Edge, isn't it?' he asked, screwing up his nose and peering closer. 'I haven't been up there for years. Been coppicing, have they?'

'Yes,' Mandy confirmed.

'Hmm,' Robbie said thoughtfully. 'Wish I'd known. I'd have gone and got some wands to make my walking-sticks. Nice pictures, lad,' he added to John, as he handed them back.

He looked slightly puzzled and obviously wondered what all the fuss was about. Had they come rushing up here just to show him some photographs? He took off his spectacles and put them back in his pocket.

'The thing is . . .' Mandy hurried to explain as she pointed to one of the pictures John was holding. 'Look at all those rabbit holes.'

'Oh, aye,' Robbie said. 'It's overrun with conies up there.'

'But we didn't see any,' John blurted out. 'Not a single one.'

'Do you think they might have been scared of the machines and deserted the warren?' Mandy asked eagerly.

Robbie looked thoughtful. 'Well . . .' he said. 'It's certainly possible.'

'So it could be just the place for *our* rabbits,' John said.

'Have the forestry chaps finished, then?' Robbie asked.

Mandy nodded. 'Yes.'

'We'd better go and look then, hadn't we?' Robbie suggested.

'Now?' John demanded.

Robbie shook his head. 'Can't go today, lad. Sorry. I've got some sticks that need finishing. They're to sell at the craft fair in Walton next week. I'm afraid it'll have to wait until tomorrow.'

'OK,' John agreed reluctantly.

They stayed a little while to watch Robbie making his sticks. Mandy admired one with a goat's head carved into the handle. She picked it up and ran her fingers over the smooth wood. The handle fitted neatly into her hand.

'When I saw that billy-goat of Lydia's I thought it looked just like him,' Robbie said.

Mandy chuckled. 'It does.'

'So I thought I might give it to her,' Robbie went on. 'Do you think she'd like it?'

'Oh, I'm sure she'd love it,' Mandy breathed.

'I will, then,' Robbie said with a grin. 'But don't you tell her,' he warned. 'It's not quite finished yet and I want it to be a surprise.'

Mandy, James and John cycled away from Lamb's Wood Cottage and towards home, already making more plans.

'If Robbie thinks Longstone Edge will be all right for the rabbits,' Mandy said, thinking of the route from Lydia's field, 'then we could ask my mum and dad to take them there in the Animal Ark Land-rover. That way, we could get the rabbits up the rough road, and right up close to the warren, all in one journey!'

'That would be great!' James was getting carried away too. 'They won't be a nuisance to *anyone* up there.' He chuckled. 'I'd love to see Sam Western's face when he finds out all the rabbits are gone.'

But John was more cautious. 'Hang on, you two,' he warned. 'Robbie's got to check the place out first.'

'That's true,' Mandy said. 'My gran always says, don't count your chickens before they're hatched.' Gran was full of sayings like that.

'Don't count your rabbits before they're moved, you mean,' James said.

And in spite of the worrying time they'd had, they all burst out laughing.

Eight

'James! John! You're here already. Great. Let's get going.' Mandy halted outside the post office the following morning where James and John were waiting with Blackie. The two boys had their boots and waterproofs on. It was a minute to eight, a misty, drizzly day; the sky heavy and grey with the threat of rain.

They made their way over to Robbie's. At Lamb's Wood Cottage he was ready and waiting, wearing a big old army great coat with huge pockets. One of them was moving!

'It's Kirsty,' Robbie explained when he saw

them staring. He opened the pocket flap and let them peer inside.

'Oh,' Mandy drew in her breath as a pair of pink eyes peered out at her. 'Is she all right in there?'

'She's fine,' Robbie assured her. 'I thought the best way to find out if there *were* any conies at Longstone Edge was to send one of my little ones down to have a look.'

'Brilliant idea!' John exclaimed.

Robbie produced a tiny little leather muzzle from one of his other pockets. 'She's been fed,' he said. 'She shouldn't be hungry but I'll put this on, just in case.' His eyes twinkled. 'We don't want any accidents, do we?'

'No,' Mandy said. 'Definitely not.'

'I've brought a couple of purse nets too,' Robbie went on. 'I'll show you how to use them.'

'Great,' James said.

A silvery mist was rising from the hillside as they made their way up to Longstone Edge. Everything was covered with moisture and drops like crystal hung from every branch and twig.

When they reached the rough track that led into the wood, Robbie stopped. 'Hmm,' he pondered, surveying the deep ruts made by the tractor tyres. 'They *have* been busy up here. I think we might be in luck. With all this going on I reckon those conies might well have decided to move house.'

Mandy ran on ahead to find one of the places where John had taken the photos. Blackie was already there, sniffing around.

When Robbie caught up, he headed for the brambles and crouched down in front of the rabbit holes. Mandy, James and John stood behind him anxiously. There was a pile of earth outside a couple of the holes.

Robbie patted it with his hand. 'This was dug some time ago. It's packed down hard. If it had been dug recently it would still be dry and crumbly.'

Mandy crouched down beside him to take a look.

'And look at those droppings,' Robbie said. 'They're not fresh either.'

Mandy wasn't sure how he could tell. Rabbit

droppings all looked the same to her. But she knew Robbie *could* tell and that was good enough for her. Her hopes were beginning to soar. No freshly dug earth, no fresh droppings: things were looking hopeful.

Robbie stood up and wandered over to a mossy bank where there were a dozen or so other holes. He stood there, studying the ground.

'What are you looking for?' James asked.

'Diggings,' Robbie replied. He crouched down. 'Rabbits are mad about digging. Moss, dirt . . . anything. And they nibble at roots and fallen branches to keep their teeth sharp.' He picked up a small branch that had been left behind by the foresters. 'Nothing on here,' he said. 'I reckon if there were conies here they'd have nibbled the bark off this by now.'

Robbie pointed out other clues. More branches and twigs lying around but none of them had teeth marks on. And there were no signs of sharp little claws digging up the moss anywhere at all.

They wandered round then came back to

where they had started, anxiously waiting for Robbie's verdict. Blackie had given up galloping about and was sniffing quietly around James's feet. Another good sign: if Blackie had discovered fresh rabbit smells he would never have given up looking for them so easily.

'Well,' Robbie said. 'It all looks pretty deserted to me, but we'd better send Kirsty down, just to make sure.' He took out the purse nets and a handful of small wooden pegs. 'I'll show you these first,' he said. He opened the net and showed them how to peg it all around the burrow entrance. 'Then when your cony comes running out he slams into the net, you grab the string and pull the ends together.' He demonstrated, pretending his hand was a rabbit. In no time at all his fingers were enclosed in the net, the strings firmly drawn up at one end. 'There you are,' he said. 'Trapped.'

'And all we'll need to do is put the rabbit in a box, bring him here and let him out,' James said.

'That's it, lad,' Robbie said. 'You've got it.'

'Seems dead easy to me,' John remarked.

Robbie shook his head. 'It's not easy at all,' he said. 'First of all we've got to make sure every single hole is covered.'

'Oh,' James said. 'There could be lots of them.'

'Right,' Robbie confirmed. 'And your rabbit will struggle like mad. Remember he'll be petrified out of his wits and desperate to escape.'

'I suppose he would be,' John commented. 'I'd be scared if someone caught me up in a net.'

Robbie smiled. 'Rabbits can be pretty strong, you know,' he said. 'And they can give you a hefty kick. It takes years to learn how to capture them skilfully.'

'But we haven't got years,' Mandy wailed. They were all aware that time was running out.

'Well, we'll just have to do the best we can then, won't we?' Robbie said with another grin.

As Robbie was talking they had been pegging and unpegging the nets to practise how to do it.

Robbie unfastened the remaining nets and put them back into his pocket. 'We don't want to catch a coney today,' he said. 'All we want to do is find out if there's any down there.'

He drew Kirsty out of his pocket. She blinked as she came out into the daylight then gave a wide yawn showing rows of sharp teeth. She sniffed the air then began wriggling to get down.

Robbie laughed. 'She knows exactly what we want her to do, don't you, my beauty?'

'She's so clever,' Mandy stroked Kirsty then held her gently while Robbie fixed on the little muzzle, doing it up gently at the back of her head. The ferret didn't seem to mind wearing it at all.

'Aye, that she is,' Robbie replied. 'But she's only using her natural hunting instincts, you know.'

'Yes,' Mandy said. 'I know that's how polecats survive in the wild.'

'Right,' Robbie said when the muzzle was firmly in place. 'Now, we need to spread out.' He pointed to the bank. 'You go there, John:

you over there, James, and you'd better tie Blackie up. If there *are* any rabbits you don't want him chasing them.'

'Right.' James did as he was told, them went to stand watch over another group of holes on the other side of the bank.

'You go over there,' Robbie told Mandy and she crashed her way through the brambles to stand on the other side. 'And keep your eyes peeled,' he called. 'They'll be out in a flash.'

When everyone was in position, Robbie bent and put Kirsty in front of a hole. 'Off you go, little one,' he murmured. Kirsty gave one more sniff then disappeared down the hole. Mandy stood well back, afraid that if a rabbit did come hurtling out it would crash into her in a panic.

'Any sign?' Robbie called to James and John. He was sitting on a log, his elbows on his knees.

James's voice came back across the clearing. 'No, none.'

Then, what seemed like hours later, John called, 'Here she is!' Kirsty had emerged from a hole by his feet.

'Pick her up,' Robbie called.

John lifted the ferret gently and brought her back to Robbie.

'Well done.' The old man's gnarled fingers smoothed the ferret's fur. 'We'll just try over here,' he said, making his way across to the end of the clearing. 'Just in case there's a separate warren.' He repeated the exercise all over again. This time, Kirsty was gone such a long time that Mandy had begun to think she'd never see her again.

Then, suddenly, James gave a shout. 'She's over there!'

They all turned to see Kirsty running around a chestnut tree fifty metres or so away.

'How on earth did she get over there?' Mandy panted as she hurried with Robbie to collect her.

'She found one of the escape routes, I expect, lass.' Robbie was out of breath too. 'Warrens always have escape routes away from the burrows so that the rabbits can get away if a predator gets in. When you're hunting you need to make sure they're covered too, otherwise you lose the lot.'

Mandy's heart turned over as she heard this. Supposing they didn't manage to find all the holes in the warren on Lydia's land? If the rabbits escaped and ended up on Sam Western's property they would be shot. She shivered, then managed to pull herself together. She had to think positively. Operation Rabbits on the Run *would* be a success. They would just have to make sure every exit was covered.

When they reached Kirsty the ferret allowed Robbie to scoop her up without any fuss. She looked a bit dirty by now, her blonde fur damp and sticky and streaked with mud.

'Good girl,' Robbie said affectionately. He removed the muzzle and put her gently back into his pocket where she curled up and went straight to sleep. 'Well, then,' he said with a broad grin. 'It looks as if we've found those old conies of yours a brand-new home.'

Mandy breathed a huge sigh of relief. Then she gave a hoot, flung her arms round Robbie and planted a huge kiss on his cheek. 'Oh, Robbie, that's brilliant! Thanks!'

James and John were grinning all over their

faces. Blackie must have known how happy they were because he started barking excitedly. James gave him a hug as untied him. 'Hear that, Blackie? Everything's going to be OK.'

But as they left Longstone Edge and headed for High Cross to tell Lydia the good news, Robbie gave them a warning. 'It's going to be tough,' he said. 'And we might not be able to get them all. But I'm sure my little ones will do their best for you.'

At High Cross, they found Lydia unloading a stack of large, sturdy cardboard boxes from the back of her old van. Mandy ran on ahead.

'Wonderful!' Lydia grinned broadly when she heard the good news. She beamed at Robbie when he came into the yard with James and John. 'I don't know what we would have done without you, Robbie.'

'Always pleased to help a lady.' Robbie bowed his head and touched the peak of his cap. 'Although you'd better wait until those rabbits are all moved before you say that.' He grinned at Lydia and winked at her.

There was a grunt and they all turned to see Ernie Bell standing in the doorway of the house, looking grumpier than ever.

'Ernie came to take a look at Houdini's shelter,' Lydia explained. 'And he's been helping me unload these boxes, haven't you, Ernie?'

'Humph,' Ernie grunted.

'Well, Ernie, old lad,' Robbie said, going to shake his hand. 'How are you keeping?'

'All right,' Ernie muttered.

John stared at the two old men. 'What's up with Ernie?' he whispered to Mandy, as Ernie took another couple of boxes from the back of the van and stomped indoors without so much as another word to Robbie. 'I thought they were friends.'

Mandy chuckled. 'I've got a feeling he didn't like that wink Robbie gave Lydia,' she said.

Lydia must have heard what she said. 'Nonsense,' she said. 'He's just in a bad mood, that's all.'

'Why?' John asked.

Lydia shrugged. 'I don't know. He was all

right until you turned up. He said it'll be no trouble at all to repair the shelter.'

'There you are, then,' Mandy said triumphantly. 'He's jealous of Robbie.'

'Nonsense,' Lydia said again as they all piled into the kitchen to finalise their rabbit rescue plans. But Mandy still chuckled to herself. She knew about Ernie's soft spot for Lydia and she had the feeling Lydia did too.

Indoors, Mandy wrote down all the names of the people they would recruit to help. Mum and Dad, Gran and Grandad, Mr and Mrs Hunter, Julian and Sara, and Simon. And herself, James and John of course. And Robbie and Lydia. Surely that would be enough people? She read the list out loud.

'You can put me down,' Ernie said. 'I'd be pleased to help.'

'Thanks, Mr Bell.' Mandy added his name. 'Right,' she said. 'We'll go and tell everyone the operation's on for tomorrow.' She beamed. 'It's going to be great ... I just can't wait! What time should I tell them to be here, Robbie?'

'The earlier the better,' he told them. 'Conies

are most active at dusk so by early morning they'll be in the warren ready for my beauties to flush them out. Seven-thirty suit you?'

'Fine,' Mandy said.

John looked doubtful. 'My dad and Sara don't usually get up that early,' he said. 'They're always late getting to bed because they have to clear up the pub when the customers have gone.'

'I'm sure they'll make a special effort.' Mandy tried to reassure him. She knew how much rescuing the rabbits meant to John.

John gave a sigh. 'I hope so.'

'Let's go and see the rabbits before we go back,' James suggested. 'We could tell *them* the good news too.'

Mandy grinned. 'Brilliant idea! Come on, John.'

They left Lydia talking to Ernie and Robbie and set off across the field.

When they reached the meadow the rabbits were out in full, the whole flick of them. Grey, tawny coats gleamed in the sun. The rabbits were nibbling and crouching, sitting up on their back legs, while the young ones played, running around with the sheer joy of being safe and free. Mandy, James and John stood there quietly, still as stones, just watching.

Mandy drew in her breath when she spotted the king rabbit sitting on a tree stump. Mandy thought she would never get tired of looking at him. He was a picture of health, bright eyes, glossy fur, big ears pink where the sun shone through the delicate skin. She held her breath as he turned. He was looking straight at her.

'I hope they'll like it in their new home,' John whispered.

'They'd better,' James said. 'After all our hard work getting things organised.'

Mandy chuckled. 'I'm sure they will,' she said.

'I wish they knew what we'd got planned for them,' John said in a wistful voice.

Mandy didn't answer. She was still staring at the king rabbit and he was still staring at her. She had a strange, uncanny feeling that he *did* know something was up. He was relaxed, yet alert at the same time. As if he was expecting something to happen although he didn't quite know what.

'Don't worry,' she whispered softly. 'It won't be long now before you'll be safe for ever.'

Nine

When they got back to the village, James and John headed home to tell their parents that Operation Rabbits on the Run was on for the following day.

Mandy was on the way to tell her gran and grandad when she caught sight of her mother's car just turning into the lane that led to Lilac Cottage, her grandparents' house.

She arrived seconds later. 'Hi, Mandy.' Emily Hope looked pleased to see her. 'Are you visiting Gran and Grandad too?'

'Yes,' Mandy replied. 'I've got something I

want to ask them . . . and you. I'll tell you when we get inside.'

Gran and Grandad were sitting at the kitchen table having a cup of tea.

'Mandy!' Gran looked surprised to see her. 'We haven't seen you at all this holiday. What have you been up to?'

Mandy gave her gran and grandad a swift hug. 'I've been meaning to come and see you but I've been so busy.'

'Doing what?' Gran asked.

'Oh, lots of things,' Mandy answered, in too much of a hurry to tell them everything she had been doing that holiday. 'But I need you and Grandad to help with something.'

She sat down and told them quickly.

Grandad shook his head when he heard about the scheme. 'I don't know, Mandy, what will you think of next?'

She leaned forward. 'But don't you see, Grandad? We've just got to save those rabbits!'

'Yes, of course, you must,' Grandad agreed hastily although he did look a bit doubtful.

'So you see,' Mandy went on, 'we're going

to need all the help we can get.'

'Including our help, you mean.' Gran put a glass of lemonade in front of Mandy and opened the biscuit tin.

Mandy took one and bit into it. 'Yes, please, Gran. And Mum.' She gazed at her mother. 'And I'm sure Dad will want to help.'

Emily Hope smiled. 'You can count me in love.'

'You did a bit of ferreting when you were a lad, didn't you, Tom?' Gran asked Grandad.

'I certainly did,' Grandad confirmed. 'Me and Ernie Bell.'

'You'll know what to do then, won't you?' Mandy said. 'Except that we're not *hunting* the rabbits, you understand.'

'Oh, I understand all right,' Grandad smiled at her. 'And, of course, I'll help you. In fact, I wouldn't miss it for the world.'

'Me neither,' Gran said.

Mandy's eyes shone. 'Thanks.'

She turned back to her mother. 'Mr Bell's offered to help. John's going to ask his dad and Sara, and James is—'

Grandad laughed. 'It sounds as if half the village will be there.'

'Not quite, Grandad,' Mandy said. 'But the more people we have, the quicker we'll be able to get it done.' She sighed. 'Mr Grimshaw said it's not going to be easy, but we've got to try, haven't we?'

Mrs Hope put an arm round her daughter's shoulders. 'We certainly have,' she said. 'Don't you worry, love. I'm sure we'll manage.'

'Yes,' Gran said. 'We must think *positively*.'

Mandy grinned. 'We are . . . so, half past seven in the morning at High Cross, OK?'

Gran looked a bit startled. 'Half past seven . . . ?'

'Of course, Dorothy,' Grandad said with a wink at Mandy. 'The early bird catches the worm, you know. That's one of your favourite sayings.'

'The early bird catches the rabbit, you mean,' Emily Hope said.

Then, as they all burst out laughing, Grandad's face suddenly fell. 'Oh dear,' he said. 'I've just remembered I'm on the rota for bell-ringing in the morning.'

'Oh!' Mandy's face fell too.

Grandad looked thoughtful. 'I could ask someone to swap . . . I'll ring Walter. He's down for evensong. I'll ask him if he'll do morning service and I'll do the evening.' Walter Pickard was another of Grandad's friends.

Mandy fidgeted impatiently while her grandfather went to phone his friend.

He came back with a grin on his face. 'No problem,' he said. 'Walter doesn't mind a bit. He'll find someone else to do the morning service with him, and then Ernie Bell and I can do the evening.'

'Brilliant!' Mandy gave her grandad a hug.

Mandy felt full of anticipation as they said goodbye. Gran was right. And so was Mum. Everything *was* going to be absolutely fine.

Back at Animal Ark, the last patient had just left. Mrs Hope went into the house and Mandy went through to help her dad clear up. When she told him of their plan he shook his head just like Grandad had. Simon was there too, listening to what she had to say.

'I don't know, Mandy,' Mr Hope said when she'd finished. 'You and your schemes.'

'You will help, though, won't you, Dad?' she asked earnestly.

He gave her a hug. 'Well, I'm supposed to be singing in the choir for morning service tomorrow, but—'

'Oh, Dad—' Mandy began.

Adam Hope grinned. 'Don't worry, I'll ring Mr Hadcroft. I'm sure they can do without me for one Sunday.' The Reverend Hadcroft was Welford's vicar. 'After all, my job is to save animals if I can,' he said. 'And that's exactly what we'll be doing.'

'You can definitely count me in too,' Simon said.

'Oh, thanks, Simon.' Mandy's eyes shone. 'That'll be brilliant.'

She went into the residential unit to see Georgie. He was looking much better already. Simon had groomed the cat's coat clean and his sore paws were healing up nicely.

'I spoke to the Wilsons,' Simon told her. 'They're coming to pick him up this afternoon.'

'That's great.' Mandy opened the cage and stroked the cat gently. 'I bet they were pleased he had turned up safe and well.' She had been so busy with the rabbit problem she had forgotten to ask before.

'They were over the moon,' Simon said with a grin.

Mandy took Georgie's bowl and filled it with fresh water. She finished her chores and then went through to the house to phone Lydia and tell her everyone had agreed to help out.

'So we're definitely all set for tomorrow?' Lydia said.

'Yes.' Mandy's heart turned over with excitement. 'See you at seven-thirty.'

'Right,' Lydia said. 'I'll be ready.'

They had just finished lunch when Simon put his head round the kitchen door. 'The Wilsons are here,' he said.

'Be right with you,' Mrs Hope replied.

Mandy followed her through to the waiting-room. A tall man wearing jeans and a dark sweatshirt and a blonde woman in a navy track suit were standing by the counter carrying a cat basket.

'Mr and Mrs Wilson,' Mrs Hope said. 'I'm so pleased you could come to collect Georgie.'

Mrs Wilson's eyes were shining. 'We couldn't believe he'd turned up,' she said smiling. 'We thought we'd never see him again.'

Mrs Hope turned to Mandy. 'Would you like to fetch him for me, Mandy?'

'He's been so clever to find his way back to Welford.' Mandy heard Mrs Wilson say, as she went through to the residential unit to fetch the cat.

She came out moments later carrying Georgie. Simon came with her to say farewell to his patient.

Mrs Wilson took her pet gently from Mandy's arms and hugged him close. 'Oh, Georgie, you are a naughty boy.' Georgie miaowed softly and rubbed his face against her neck, obviously overjoyed to see his mistress again. Mrs Wilson looked at everyone with tears in her eyes. 'Thank you so much for looking after him.'

Mr Wilson took Georgie gently from his wife's

arms and cuddled him. 'Don't ever scare us like that again!' he said.

Mrs Hope warned them about keeping Georgie in for a few days. 'Once he knows where his food and his bed are he won't stray again,' she told them.

They all went out to the Wilsons' car to say goodbye. Mandy gave a little sigh as they drove off down the lane, Georgie tucked away safely in the back in his basket.

'Another satisfied customer.' Mrs Hope smiled.

'I hope Georgie settles down at his new house this time,' Mandy said.

'I'm sure he will,' her mum assured her, 'now that the Wilsons know what to do.'

Mandy gave a sigh. 'And I hope the rabbits settle down in their new home too.'

Her mum gave her a quick hug. 'So do I, love,' she replied.

Mandy felt a sudden surge of excitement. If everything went according to plan, by this time tomorrow the rabbits would be in their new home at Longstone Edge.

She just couldn't wait!

Ten

On Sunday morning, Mandy was up long before her alarm went off. She could already hear someone moving around in the bathroom. Then she heard her mum go downstairs. She threw back the duvet, leaped out of bed and pulled back the curtains. Today was the day. Operation Rabbits on the Run! She felt a tight knot of excitement in her stomach as she dragged on jeans and a sweatshirt.

The sun wasn't up yet and a mist still lay over the garden and the lane beyond. She opened the window and took a breath of mild, fresh air.

Downstairs, Emily Hope was getting the breakfast although Mandy felt too full of anticipation to be hungry.

'You must eat something,' her mum insisted. 'We've got some hard work ahead of us today and you'll need lots of energy.'

Sitting at the table, Mandy suddenly found she *was* hungry and wolfed down her cereal and toast.

Adam Hope came into the kitchen looking a bit bleary-eyed, just as Mandy was pushing her feet into her boots. Then Simon appeared. He had spent the night in the spare room so he would be there bright and early too.

'Come on, you two!' Mandy exclaimed impatiently. 'I'm ready and you haven't even had breakfast.'

Mr Hope and Simon were just shovelling down a bowl of cereal each when there was a knock at the door. James and his parents stood there. They had thought it wise to leave Blackie behind.

James glanced at his watch. 'Aren't you ready yet? It's time to go.'

'Nearly,' Mandy said. She turned to her dad and Simon. 'Please hurry up, you two!'

Mr Hope and Simon finished their breakfast and got on their boots and jackets. Mrs Hope had gone to start the Land-rover.

James's parents drove behind the Animal Ark Land-rover up the lane towards the village, and as they reached the green, they saw Gran and Grandad's camper van coming down the road to meet them. Ernie Bell was with them too, and Mandy and James turned to give them a thumbs-up sign as they followed the other two vehicles towards the High Street.

Mr and Mrs Hunter stopped to pick up John, Julian and Sara at the Fox and Goose, then the convoy drove towards High Cross.

When they arrived, Robbie was already there. He and Lydia had piled the cardboard boxes outside ready to put them into the back of the Land-rover.

Mandy thrust open the Land-rover door,

jumped out and ran over to them. She saw that Robbie had the ferrets in little carrying cages.

Lydia was looking very pleased with herself as she greeted them all. 'Look at this,' she said proudly. The goat's head walking-stick was in her hand. 'Isn't it beautiful?'

Robbie had varnished the walking-stick a deep chestnut brown and the goat's head looked amazingly lifelike. It fitted perfectly into Lydia's small hand.

'It's wonderful,' Mrs Hope said admiringly.

'Robbie made it,' Mandy told her. 'Isn't he clever?'

'He certainly is,' her mum agreed.

Ernie was standing by the camper. 'Look, Ernie,' Lydia showed him the stick.

Ernie couldn't help admiring it too. 'Hmm,' he said grudgingly. 'You always were clever with your hands, Robbie Grimshaw.'

'Aye,' Robbie agreed. 'I can carve. But I'm no carpenter, Ernie. That's where you come into your own.'

Then Mandy noticed that Houdini's shelter

had been repaired. The roof was straight and the side was mended.

'Ernie stayed and did it yesterday afternoon,' Lydia explained. 'It's as good as new.'

'That's great, Mr Bell,' Mandy said. She couldn't help chuckling to herself. Ernie had done a good job but it was a very long time since Houdini's shelter had looked like new!

Lydia smiled at Ernie. 'I don't know what I'd have done without you, Ernie.'

Ernie looked pleased when she said that. He took the walking-stick from her hand and looked closer. Then he handed it back. 'Nice,' he said. 'Very nice indeed.' The next moment he was helping Robbie put the ferret cages and boxes into the back of the Hopes' vehicle.

Mandy and Lydia grinned at each other.

Lydia shook her head. 'Those two,' she said, laughing.

John was shuffling his feet anxiously. 'Isn't it about time we got going?'

'It certainly is,' Robbie said. 'Come on, everyone. Let's go.'

Mandy's knees were wobbly with excitement

as she went with John and Robbie to open the gate.

'It's going to be brilliant, isn't it, Mr Grimshaw?' John said excitedly as they stood back to let the Land-rover through.

'It might be brilliant to you, lad,' Robbie said. 'But it's going to be hard work.'

'I don't care,' John declared.

Robbie couldn't help smiling at John's eager face. 'Aye, lad,' he said. 'Neither do I.'

Lydia's goats skipped away bleating as the Land-rover came through. Mrs Hope drove carefully across the paddock and came to a halt by the far gate. Lydia strode behind with the others, her walking-stick in her hand.

Mrs Hope cut the engine and climbed out, then Mandy and Grandad began unloading the boxes. Adam Hope picked up a couple, then went with Robbie over the stile to take the ferrets to the edge of the warren. The rabbits had already scattered and disappeared as soon as they heard the vehicle's engine and the thump of human footsteps on the turf.

Robbie took bundles of purse nets and

handed them round. Everyone spread out, pegging the nets round entrances to every hole they could find. John went with his father and Sara to show them how to do it and James did the same with his parents. Grandad went along with Gran, Mr Hope and Simon.

'Don't miss any,' Robbie called.

Just under an hour later, every hole they could find was covered. Mandy and James had even found the escape routes by crawling around in the undergrowth until they located them. Everyone assembled back with Robbie and the ferrets.

'Right, everybody,' Robbie said. 'Try to keep calm. The less noise we make, the better.' He took Marlon from his little cage and stroked his back. John held him while Robbie fixed on the muzzle. Then he bent, undid a corner of one of the purse nets and pushed Marlon through the gap. Then he did the same with Kirsty and Sable. Soon all three ferrets had disappeared.

Marlon hadn't been gone more than a minute or two when the first rabbit appeared, hurtling in panic to slam into the net by John's feet.

'Here's one!' he shouted, so excited he had forgotten all about Robbie's warning to keep calm.

Robbie hurried over. 'Right, lad,' he said. 'You know what to do.'

John had already pulled the strings and caught the rabbit fast in the net. It was struggling frantically, its dark eyes wide with fear. Robbie helped him undo the net and transfer the squirming creature to one of the boxes. 'Make sure the box is properly closed,' he warned. 'We don't want them jumping out!'

Before long it seemed to Mandy that the ground was alive with snared, struggling rabbits. They were picked up and carried to the back of the Land-rover where Robbie and Simon gently released them and placed them in the boxes. The nets were then quickly repegged over the holes.

Suddenly, Gran gave a shout. 'Someone help, please!' Simon went running across. Gran had a rabbit caught up in the net and was having trouble releasing it. With the help of Simon's gentle hands the rabbit was soon free.

Simon carried her to the back of the vehicle while Gran quickly repegged the net round the entrance. No sooner had she done so than another rabbit appeared. Gran pulled the strings, unpegged the net deftly and took the rabbit over to Robbie.

He winked at her. 'I could have done with someone like you to help me when I was a young man,' he told her.

Gran chuckled. 'Get away with you, you old scoundrel,' she said, laughing.

Out of the corner of her eye Mandy saw John sprawled on the ground and ran to help. He had two rabbits tangled together in one net. They were both struggling madly, desperate to escape. She helped John carry them back to the Land-rover. Robbie managed to get one free and put it quickly into a box. The other one had stopped struggling. When Robbie freed it, it lay limply in his hands, its eyes open wide.

Mandy held her breath. 'Is it dead?'

'No, lass,' Robbie said. 'Rabbits freeze like

that sometimes. It's just frightened out of its wits.'

'Poor thing,' Mandy murmured as Robbie placed the scared creature into a box.

'It'll be fine, I'm sure,' he told her.

Then she heard the scrabble of claws against cardboard from inside and heaved a sigh of relief.

Reassured, she ran off to help James. She had spotted him diving after a rabbit that was managing to scramble away with the net still attached to its neck and forelegs.

'It's gone into the maize,' James panted as Mandy arrived.

'Then we'd better go after it,' she said. She got on her hands and knees, crawled under the wire fence and into the forest of tall maize stalks. Sharp-edged leaves snagged at her hair and face as she screwed up her eyes, trying to locate the rabbit. Then she saw it, a little way ahead, still struggling to run. She saw it fall, its back legs kicking. Her heart thudded. Supposing the rabbit had injured itself in its desperate attempt to escape?

'Can you see it?' James was behind her, straightening his glasses where the plants had knocked them askew.

'Yes.' Mandy pushed her way towards the rabbit and scooped it up. She held it close to her chest as she crawled backwards and out into the air again.

'Is it OK?' James asked anxiously.

'I'm not sure,' Mandy said. The rabbit had stopped struggling and she could feel its warm body against her sweatshirt, its tiny heart thumping frantically against hers. 'Come on, little one,' she said. 'Let's get you back with your friends.' Her heart was in her mouth as she carried it carefully back to Robbie.

He confirmed the rabbit was all right.

Then came a shout from Sara. 'One's got away!' Mandy looked up and saw a youngster dashing away and disappearing rapidly into the maize field with a flick of its tail. Julian had started to run after it but had stopped, knowing he'd never catch it.

Mandy stood up, her hands on her hips. 'Oh,

no!' She turned to Robbie in a panic. 'Robbie, what can we do?'

He shook his head. 'Nothing, I'm afraid, lass. There's bound to be one or two that escape. It's no good worrying about them.' And as he spoke another rabbit darted away after the first one. It had run from the hole before Ernie could renew one of the nets.

Mandy stared at the escaping rabbits for a second or two then turned back to the task in hand. Robbie was right, some were bound to get away. All she could hope was that they'd find a new home for themselves far away from Sam Western's land.

It was nearly two hours later, when Mandy felt she was just about to collapse with exhaustion, that everything suddenly went quiet. She looked up to see Robbie holding Marlon and Sable, one ferret in each hand. The back of the Land-rover was packed with boxes full of rabbits, two or three in each one, crouched in the dark, confused and scared but secure.

'I think that might be all,' Robbie said softly,

and as everyone looked round there wasn't a rabbit to be seen anywhere.

But where was Kirsty? Mandy realised she hadn't seen her for ages.

They all stood there, waiting. Mandy had re-pegged a net round a hole by her feet. She was just beginning to relax, to really believe they had them all when a grey shape hurtled out. Hot on its heels came Kirsty, her sharp teeth snapping harmlessly inside the muzzle. Mandy bent swiftly to draw the strings of the net together and gather up the struggling animal. Robbie came to scoop Kirsty up from the ground.

Mandy held the rabbit to her chest while, with difficulty, she began to release the strings and untangle the net from the rabbit's claws. It took her longer this time. This rabbit seemed to be much bigger and stronger than the others she had handled earlier. Then, suddenly, it stopped struggling. Mandy finished removing the rabbit from its net, then drew in her breath. The rabbit was indeed much bigger than the other rabbits. Bigger and glossier. It was the one she had named the king. He had stayed until last, defending his warren from the invading ferrets until he too felt compelled to flee.

Mandy stroked his head and murmured soothing words. 'Don't worry,' she said. 'No one's going to hurt you.'

She carried him to the Land-rover and put him into the last empty box. He was so big he almost filled it up all on his own. She secured the flaps together at the top.

'Right,' Robbie said from behind her. 'Well done, lass. I think that's all. Let's go. The quicker we get them to Longstone Edge, the better.'

Mandy got into the Land-rover beside Mrs Hope. Her eyes were shining. 'Mum, wasn't that brilliant?'

'Brilliant,' Emily Hope repeated with a wry smile. Wearily she drew a muddy hand across her brow. Her face was streaked with dirt and her jeans and jacket were filthy. Mandy was the same and so was everyone else. Grandad had torn his trousers, Gran's hair was full of leaves and twigs, Mrs Hunter's hands were scratched and Ernie looked like a scarecrow. But no one

seemed to care a bit. The rabbits were safe, that was all that mattered.

The others followed on foot, across the goat paddock.

As the party made its way back, Mandy spotted a new vehicle parked in Lydia's yard. 'Oh, no,' Mandy said. 'That's Mr Western! What's he doing here?'

Sam Western was standing in the yard staring in surprise at the convoy of muddy, tired-looking people tramping across the field towards him.

John opened the gate for Mrs Hope and she drove the Land-rover through and stopped.

'Good morning.' Sam Western said to Lydia.

'Can I help you?' she asked without replying to his greeting.

Mandy and Mrs Hope had got down from the vehicle and were standing beside her.

'Emily,' Sam Western nodded to Mandy's mum. 'Adam.'

'Morning, Sam,' Mandy's dad said cheerfully. 'Nice morning.' Mrs Hope nodded and the others did the same.

Then Sam Western seemed to notice Robbie putting his carrying cages into the back of Mr Hunter's car. He eyed the boxes stacked in the back of the Land-rover. 'What's going on?' he asked suspiciously.

'What business is it of yours?' Lydia asked before anyone else could answer.

'Er . . . none, I suppose,' Sam Western conceded with a shrug.

'If you must know . . .' Lydia began. Mandy held her breath. Surely Lydia wasn't going to tell Mr Western what they had been up to? '. . . my friends are here for a visit,' Lydia said. 'And Mr Grimshaw has been showing us his pets.'

Mandy almost giggled out loud. Lydia had given Sam Western a perfectly truthful explanation. Behind her, she heard James and John give muffled snorts of laughter.

Sam Western frowned. 'Well . . .' he said. 'Anyway, I came to check that you realise the court order is in force from tomorrow.'

'Yes, of course I realise it,' Lydia said. 'I may live up here alone, Mr Western, but I do know what day of the week it is.'

'Good old Lydia,' James whispered.

'Then my men and I will be here first thing in the morning,' Sam Western said.

'That's fine,' Lydia said calmly. 'Come at whatever time you like.'

Sam Western swallowed. 'Oh . . . er . . . right.'

'But don't scare my goats with your guns,' she warned. 'If they stop producing milk I'll expect compensation.'

Sam Western didn't answer. It was obvious he couldn't understand Lydia's attitude. He clearly expected her to make some kind of a fuss.

'Er . . . right,' he said again. He got into his vehicle and slammed the door.

Everyone waited while he turned on the ignition, started the engine and drove rapidly through the gate and away down the hill. Then they turned to one another and burst out laughing.

Lydia wiped her eyes. 'I'd love to see their faces when they turn up in the morning and there's no rabbits to shoot.'

'Me too,' Mandy chuckled.

'Right,' Robbie said. 'Let's go, shall we?'

When they reached Longstone Edge they left the cars at the start of the foresters' road and followed the Land-rover on foot. Mandy was in the front seat with her mother. There wasn't a sound from the rabbits in the back. Mandy hoped they were all right. She knew they were confused and frightened, crouching in the dark, wondering what on earth was going on.

The vehicle bumped slowly over the ruts and came to a halt at the edge of the clearing. Mandy jumped out and opened the back. She began carefully unloading the boxes.

When the others caught up they helped carry the boxes to the clearing.

'Shall we open them one at a time?' John asked. His face was flushed with excitement.

'No, best open as many as we can at once,' Robbie said. 'Then they'll know they're not on their own.'

'Right,' Mandy said when they were all crouched and ready. 'Now!'

They pulled open the box flaps and soon the ground was covered with fleeing rabbits. Tails bobbing, hind legs kicking, they fanned out, running in all direction. Then one located a hole and disappeared, then another and another. Some ran off into the wood, others scrambled beneath brambles in their panic to get under cover. In no time at all there wasn't a rabbit to be seen.

There was only one box left. As Mandy began to open it she realised it was the one containing the king rabbit.

Mandy carefully tipped it on to its side. 'Off you go,' she whispered. 'Good luck . . . keep safe.'

The huge rabbit scrambled out. He didn't run in panic like the others. He crouched in front of Mandy for a moment, huddled and still afraid. Then he sat up on his hind legs and looked around. His black nose twitched as he sniffed the air, then in one bound he was away, running as fast as he could towards the nearest hole. At the entrance he turned, gave them all a brief, proud stare, then disappeared in a flick of white. Everyone stood there, not saying a word as silence settled around the clearing. Then, in the distance, a blackbird began to sing and a few leaves came fluttering down at their feet.

Mandy was the first one to speak. 'That's it,' she exclaimed triumphantly. 'That's all of them.'

James let out a great cheer and they all hugged one another and clapped each other on the back. John danced round the clearing with Sara. Julian and Mr Hunter shook hands as Mrs Hope and Lydia gave one another a big hug. Simon looked as pleased as punch and Robbie and Ernie just stood there, beaming at each other but not saying a word.

'Thank you *so* much, everyone,' Mandy's eyes were shining. It had been wonderful watching the rabbits run to safety. She knew she would never forget it.

She went to Robbie and gave him a hug. 'Thanks, Robbie, we could never have done it without you.'

Robbie touched the peak of his old cap. 'That's all right, lass,' he said, a smile splitting his old face in two. 'You're very welcome.'

As everyone walked back to the cars talking excitedly, Mandy stood still for a moment. The breeze rustled the trees and overhead she could hear pigeons cooing in the branches. She gave a sigh of satisfaction. Longstone Edge had been the perfect safe place for Lydia's rabbits to run to. She wouldn't ever have to worry about them again.

HORSE IN THE HOUSE
Animal Ark 37

Lucy Daniels

Mandy Hope loves animals more than anything else. She knows quite a lot about them too: both her parents are vets and Mandy helps out in their surgery, Animal Ark.

Mandy and James are sad when old Wilfred Bennett has to sell his riding stables and Sam Western turns the land into a campsite. But the campers are soon telling stories of a ghostly horse and rider passing by – then vanishing into the night air! Mandy and James don't believe the spooky tales – but what's *really* going on?